THE PHANTOM CYCLIST

and Other Ghost Stories

THE
PHANTOM CYCLIST
and other ghost stories

Ruth Ainsworth

Line drawings by Antony Maitland
Jacket painting by Mike Eagle

Follett Publishing Company

Chicago

ISBN 0–695–80461–8 Trade binding
ISBN 0–695–40461–X Titan binding

Library of Congress Catalog Card Number: 73–90057

Second Printing

Contents

The Phantom Cyclist

Roger and Sam were friends. They lived in the same village by the sea, surrounded by flat salt marshes and swept by a ceaseless wind. They spent every spare minute together and found a surprising number of interesting, and even exciting, things to do in the lonely village that strangers described as "dead and alive."

They lay in the reeds and watched wild birds through a pair of binoculars belonging to Sam's father: oyster catchers and terns and sheld-ducks. They knew where the sea asters grew, and the sea arrow-grass and the glasswort. They could find their way across the ever-changing channels of water, knowing when it was safe to wade and when it was wiser to walk on a mile or two and cross by a bridge, which was often only a slippery plank.

But best of all, they each had a new bicycle. Their birthdays happened to be in the same month, so they acquired their bicycles almost at the same time. The bicycles differed in color, Roger's being green and Sam's purple. But they had many good points in common. They were racing bicycles, and each had a five-speed gear, cable brakes, a holder for a bottle of pop, and a hooter guaranteed to scare old ladies or stray chickens.

As there were no movies, skating rinks, or other forms of entertainment for many miles, their parents spent a great deal of money on the bicycles, and they did not regret this as their sons sped off, day after day, armed with a bottle of drink and a picnic, and seemed to be perfectly happy just cycling around the flat, deserted countryside.

One Friday after school, when the days were beginning to draw in, Roger suggested a quick spin to the tower and back, a distance of about four miles in all.

The wind was behind them, and they had a friendly race along the empty road, sometimes Roger drawing ahead, and then Sam overtaking him. Suddenly, with no warning at all, a boy dressed in white, white shirt and white shorts and white gym shoes, drew level. He was riding an old-fashioned bicycle with upright handlebars. Both Roger and Sam put their heads down and pressed on with all possible speed, as being passed by another cyclist, especially a boy, challenged them to do their best. But the white-clad boy overtook them easily and forged ahead. They lost sight of him when the road curved inland and went over a bridge across a deep channel known as Devil's Dike.

As they crossed the bridge themselves, they looked in vain for the cyclist on the other side. But they could see no trace of him.

"He can't have gotten so far in front; it isn't possible," said Roger. The two stopped for a minute on the bridge, leaning on the iron railings without getting off their bikes.

"White shows up so clearly. Look at that white cow over there. She must be a mile away or more. We can see her."

"He must have gotten off the road for some reason," said Roger. "Perhaps he's got a puncture. This is a pretty rough, stony surface."

"I rather hope he *has* got into some trouble," said Sam, wishing the unknown boy no ill. "I'd love to have a close look at that bike of his. It must be a miracle."

"Yes, but I thought it looked kind of old-fashioned, what I could see of it."

"Let's go on. If he's having any trouble with his bike, we shall pass him between here and the tower. We must pass him. Perhaps we could give him a hand. Maybe his chain has come off. Remember how mine used to come off till Dad took a link out and tightened it?"

They rode on, no longer hurrying, and scanning the grass verges as they went. Eventually the tower came into sight, a bare, circular building where they had often played and lit fires and had picnics.

But it was too late to play now. They got off and walked around the tower and then turned back for home. The wind was in their faces this time and they had to pedal harder. Conversation was almost impossible as the wind whirled their words away. They reached Sam's house first, and stopped at his gate for a last chat.

"I can't understand it," said Roger. "I simply can't undertstand. I suppose a very fit cyclist could have overtaken us—just barely—but where did he disappear to? We never saw him after he'd turned inland towards Devil's Dike Bridge, and he couldn't have gone any other way because there isn't any other way to go. The dike must be ten feet wide, perhaps more, and there's no side turning anywhere. The track to Devil's Farm doesn't lead off till just opposite the tower."

"He must be very eager to be training at this time of day and in this wind," added Sam. "Those white things he was wearing were like .the things racing cyclists wear—a shirt and shorts. Perhaps he's training to be a road racer."

"I've never heard of a famous boy cyclist, though I don't see why boys shouldn't be famous racers. I'd like to be one. I may be when I'm grown-up."

"I thought you were going to be a vet."

"Well, so I am, but I can do cycle racing in my spare time."

"You won't get much spare time if you're studying to be a vet. Mother says it takes as long learning to be a vet as learning to be a real doctor."

"It *is* being a real doctor, silly, only you don't treat people. It's harder than being a people's doctor. You have to know about birds' skeletons and reptiles and everything. Think of all the creatures in a zoo and all the queer pets people keep. Vets must know how to treat them all."

Both boys could not forget the strange cyclist in white who had sped past them at such an amazing speed. The way that he had disappeared into thin air was particularly puzzling. If only they'd had a proper look at him and his bicycle. But they hadn't had a chance.

Roger and Sam kept up their habit of riding around after school, but they never came across any strangers cycling on the road. An occasional van or a farmer in a Land-Rover sometimes passed them. The only regular cyclist was Meg, the postwoman, who cycled everywhere, in all weather, like themselves.

A week went by, and they began to think less about the mysterious boy. Saturday was clear and sunny, and they decided to take a picnic to the old quarry. It had not been worked for many years, and was a good place to play in. They could climb on the rocky faces and sometimes find a stone marked long ago by the drill.

It was sheltered, too, and very fine blackberries could be found there. Their mothers had given them each a plastic bag on the chance that a few late berries would still be left, enough for a blackberry and apple pie on Sunday.

One of the few hills in the district, Shottery Hill, led up to the quarry. This gave them much-needed practice in hill-climbing, and they took great pride in getting up without a rest, however much their muscles ached.

When they reached the quarry, they immediately noticed a bicycle propped against a rock. It was black and very out-of-date with mud-guards covering half the wheels and straight handlebars. They were not sur-

prised to see the mysterious boy in white eating blackberries a few yards away. He was dressed in the same
white short-sleeved shirt and rather long, baggy shorts.

"Are there many blackberries?" asked Roger.

"Quite a few, here and there."

"We're supposed to pick enough for a pie. Well, for
two pies." He produced his plastic bag.

"I'll help you. They need searching for."

Sam got his bag out of his pocket, too, and the three
boys picked steadily. The strange boy put a handful
sometimes in Roger's bag and sometimes in Sam's. He
was very fair and pale and thin. His arms were like
sticks and had no trace of tan on them. For an athletic
type he appeared fragile.

"You get along fast on that bike of yours," said
Roger. "Sam and I thought you were pretty good when
you passed us on the coast road the other evening."

"We were going flat out," added Sam, "but you left
us miles behind."

"Wherever did you get to when you rounded the
bend to Devil's Bridge? You weren't in sight when we
got there."

"I just went over the bridge and on," said the boy.
"The way I always go."

"But you couldn't—" began Roger, and stopped. "I
mean, it was odd how you disappeared. We waited on
the bridge for ages."

The boy looked up with interest.

"You waited *on* the bridge?"

"Yes, we leaned against the railings and looked for
you."

"There was nothing to be seen except a white cow," said Sam.

"But I don't see how you could have waited *on* the bridge, both of you. It's only a single plank. I get into trouble for riding over it instead of getting off and pushing my bike over."

"Trouble from your parents, you mean?"

"I haven't any parents. Trouble from my uncle and aunt who have brought me up. They don't want me to slip when the plank is muddy or frosty."

"I don't think we're talking about the same thing," said Roger. "The bridge we went over is quite wide—a car can go over—and there are railings on each side painted white. That's to help people to see them in the dark."

"No, we're not talking about the same thing," said the boy sadly. "We can't ever talk about the same thing."

He looked so upset that both Roger and Sam felt they must try to cheer him up. They could discuss the bridge—or was it the bridges?—afterwards.

"Thanks awfully for the blackberries. I'm Roger and he's Sam. Who are you?"

"I'm Per. My mother was Norwegian. That's why I'm so fair. And Per is a Norwegian name."

"May we look at your bike, Per? The brake looks queer to me. How does it work?"

Per quickly showed them how the brake worked on the front wheel, but you had to pedal backwards to stop the back wheel. "It's called a back-pedaling brake," he explained.

"Let's have a game, Per. You and Sam go and hide, and I'll count a hundred slowly and then come and look for you. All right?"

Per scaled the rocky face with such skill and speed that Sam found it was all he could do to follow. They flattened themselves in a crack and Roger passed them twice before he caught sight of Per's white shirt.

"That was a fabulous place. I thought I knew the quarry inside out, but I'd never noticed that crevice. Now Sam and I'll hide and you count a hundred."

Roger and Sam hid in one of their favorite spots, a hollow filled with bushes and bracken. But they didn't fool Per for long. He seemed drawn to the hollow like a dog following a scent.

"Have you been here before, Per?"

"Yes and no."

"Well, it must be one or the other."

"Yes, then. But I couldn't go just anywhere like we can today. Then men wouldn't let me. I had to dodge them all the time. The foreman was a brute. He called me 'a dirty foreigner' when he caught sight of me once. I took care he never caught sight of me again."

Per was agile as an acrobat, and when the boys began to do handstands and cartwheels on a smooth stretch of turf, he outshone them both. Feats which they had practiced for hours Per learned in a jiffy and performed with ease. He seemed absolutely unaware of his gifts and became uneasy when the others praised him. He turned aside and a tinge of color crept into his pale cheeks.

Roger and Sam shared their picnic with Per, and he

enjoyed the cheese sandwiches and apple patties and chocolate.

"My aunt never gave me anything like this," he remarked, biting into an apple patty. "Great slabs of dry bread and a sliver of meat, that's all I ever got."

"You've grown very strong on it," said Roger. "Your muscles must be terrific."

When they left to go home, Per was unwilling to cycle with them.

"You go on," he said. "I've something I want to do to my bike."

"Then we'll wait," said Roger. "Are you coming our way? Back to Welland Village?"

"As a matter of fact, I don't think I am. My way home is different. Good-bye."

"Good-bye, Per. We'll see you sometime."

"Good-bye. Thanks for the picnic."

Roger and Sam cycled slowly, hoping that Per might overtake them. There were so many questions they wanted to ask, but they did not know if they could be answered.

That evening, when Roger's father had come home from work for his supper, Roger said to him suddenly: "Was the quarry working when you were a boy, Dad?"

"No, son. It was derelict as it is now. A little less overgrown, perhaps. Me and my pals played there like you and Sam do."

"Was it working when your father was a boy?"

His father paused. "I believe it was, but my dad didn't work there. He went back to the land and was a stockman at Sunnyacre Farm. He died when I was still at school, you know, gored by a bull. But when my granddad was a lad, he worked there. He worked there till he retired. Pretty well all the men around here had jobs in the quarry in those days. There wasn't anything else to do, except for farm work. There isn't much else now, come to that. Most men have jobs away from Welland, in the town, same as me."

"Was that a hundred years ago?"

Again his father paused. "Not quite. I reckon it was about eighty years when he started working there. Children left school at twelve in those days."

"We've got an old photo of your granddad," said Roger's mother. "You know, the one taken when the men had a holiday for some occasion, like Queen Victoria's death. I'll get it."

She rummaged in a drawer and brought out a rather yellow print of a group of men. Many of them wore beards or moustaches, and they were arranged like a school photograph: the back row stood on something, the next row stood on their own feet, and the front row sat, or sprawled, on the grass. In the center, on a chair, sat an old gentleman in a top hat and frock coat.

"Where's great-grandfather?" asked Roger.

"The one in the back row with the very bushy beard."

"And who's the chap in the middle in the funny hat?"

"Oh, I guess he was the owner of the quarry, the boss, in fact."

Roger looked intently at his great-grandfather, and then at his father.

"He has curly hair like you, Dad. Do you think you could grow a curly beard, if you tried?"

"Well, he's not going to try," said his mother sharply. "Nasty, bristly, unhygienic things."

"I shall grow one when I'm old enough," said Roger, stroking his smooth, round chin. "I think I should look smashing. When can I have an electric razor and start shaving, Dad?"

"Oh, in another six or seven years, perhaps."

The next few weeks passed without either of the boys coming across Per. They cycled to the tower and to the quarry, but they never met him, though they talked about him almost all the time they were together. Where had he gone the evening he'd passed them on the coast road? Where was the single plank that he had mentioned, spanning the Devil's Dike? How could he have visited the quarry and found it full of men working, when there hadn't been work done there for years and years? Although they came to no conclusions, they could not leave the subject alone. It fascinated them.

Every Thursday evening, after school, Roger cycled into the next village for his music lesson. It lay between Welland and the big town of Queen's Lynn. It was getting dark earlier now, and he had to have his lights on for the homeward trip.

His violin teacher was an old man who had once

been a professional violinist, but was now poor and forgotten. Roger's parents often told him how lucky he was to have such a famous musician for a teacher, and Mr. Pirelli agreed with them. He, too, thought Roger was lucky. The only person in any doubt about his good fortune was Roger himself. Mr. Pirelli had fierce white eyebrows, piercing black eyes which rolled in anger when Roger played a wrong note, and thin, yellow hands from which Roger shrank when they touched him.

He had a blistering tongue which almost reduced Roger to tears. No one likes to be called "a deaf donkey" or "an imbecile" or "an uncouth peasant" and other names. But Roger bore all these indignities because he loved his violin and wanted to play well. He still had hopes of being a vet *and* a racing cyclist *and* a famous violinist. Time would show if he could manage to achieve all three ambitions.

On this particular Thursday Roger had passed the quarry, which was on the way to Mr. Pirelli's cottage, and was about two miles from the cottage itself, when he made a horrifying discovery. He had forgotten his music case. It was still on the chair in the hall at home. His violin was safe enough, strapped on his back, but the thought of appearing before Mr. Pirelli without his music was frightening. Should he go home and say he was ill? Should he go back for his music and be late for his lesson? Should he just turn up without his music?

None of these possible courses of action appealed.

Once before he had forgotten his music and Mr. Pirelli had been in a blazing temper and kept him on scales and exercises for the entire lesson.

Just then he found Per beside him. He had not heard him coming, but he was delighted to see him. He poured out all his troubles into Per's sympathetic ear. Per never hesitated a second.

"I'll go back and fetch your music and catch up with you. You just ride on. You say it's the white cottage with the fir tree by the gate? I'll be there as soon as you are."

"But Per, you can't be. It's at least two miles back. That's six altogether. I'll be so late it won't be worth turning up at all."

"I'll be quicker than you think. Please trust me. Can I get your music easily?"

"Yes, of course. Just open the door, and it's on the chair in the hall. But Per—"

"No time for 'buts.' Now ride on and don't worry. I know a shortcut. Good-bye."

Per was dressed in his usual outfit of shirt and shorts and gym shoes, and he flashed out of sight. Roger, puzzled but nevertheless relieved, cycled briskly on. As he dismounted by the fir tree and propped up his bicycle, there was a rush of wind and Per jammed on his brakes and drew up beside him. He handed over the music case, smiled, and rode away. Roger knocked on the door, his hand shaking slightly.

The lesson went unusually well. Mr. Pirelli told several amusing stories of his own young days, and actually said, "Bravo! Not bad, my young maestro!" when Roger played his Chopin study.

He could hardly wait to see Sam the next day and to tell him of the incident. Sam was a real friend and always listened and believed what he was told, however incredible it sounded.

"So Per cycled roughly four miles in the time you took to cycle two, and went into your house for the music," said Sam.

"Yes. I swear he did."

"And you didn't kind of dawdle?"

"No, I rode quickly. Quite up to my normal speed."

"That shortcut Per mentioned. Do you know where it could have been?"

"I've no idea. But I do know this: there's no track between Mr. Pirelli's cottage and our house except the road."

"But there may have been once. That's the point. Do you think we could get hold of some old maps? We might be able to find a footpath or something over the marshes."

"Yes, we might."

Just then the bell rang for the end of the morning break, and the children ran in from the playground, Roger and Sam with them.

"There's only one thing to do," said Roger after school. "We must go to see Mr. Penrose and ask if we can look at some of his old maps. He's got old maps simply everywhere. He's got one on the wall that shows wrecks and mermaids and a spouting whale."

"Let's go after tea. He's always glad to see people now that his rheumatism is bad and he can't get about."

All the village loved Mr. Penrose. He had been vicar of Welland Church some years ago, and had christened most of the children's fathers and mothers, and married them, too. He was gentle and friendly, with none of the alarming habits of Mr. Pirelli.

The two boys rang Mr. Penrose's bell that very evening, having assured both sets of parents that they had done their homework. No one thought it at all strange that they should visit Mr. Penrose. He was an authority on birds' eggs, wild flowers, fossils, locomotives, vintage cars, in fact on all subjects that interest young people.

At their request for old maps of the district, Mr. Penrose opened a cupboard door and revealed a wonderful collection of maps, some in the flat binding of the Ordinance Survey Maps, and some on rolled sheets of paper.

"How far back do you want to go? The vicar before me was somewhat of an expert on maps and he bequeathed me his collection. 1800? 1900?"

"Sort of in between."

"What about this—printed about 1870. Let's spread it out on the desk."

Mr. Penrose soon saw where the boys' interests lay. Guided by him, they discovered a track from Mr. Pirelli's cottage to Welland, going straight across the marshes, like the third side of a triangle, the present road forming the other two sides. They found no signs of the coast road as they knew it, only a faint track which seemed to cross Devil's Dike.

"There must have been a footbridge here, perhaps just a plank," said Mr. Penrose, "because the track goes on on the far side. If you wanted to drive cows across, or a wagon, you'd have to go several miles inland and cross by the bridge we still use."

The boys studied the map with great care, identifying familiar landmarks like the church and the tower, and noticing paths and tracks which no longer existed, now overgrown or covered by water.

"Why this sudden interest in maps?" asked Mr. Penrose casually, and the boys knew he would not press them if they did not choose to answer.

"Let's tell him," said Roger suddenly.

"Yes, let's."

Between them, they told Mr. Penrose everything they knew about Per and of their three meetings with him. Each kept chipping in with some extra detail, and sometimes both talked together, but Mr. Penrose did not appear to find the story confusing. He just nodded encouragingly when there was a pause. At the end, he rolled up the map carefully before he spoke.

"Now I'm going to tell you a story, as strange and true as the one you have told me. You've seen the memorial stone in the seawall?"

"Yes, lot's of times."

"What does it say?"

"This is to commemorate the men, women, **and**

children who lost their lives in the high tide of 1898. Underneath are the everlasting arms."

"Good, Sam. You've a useful memory that will serve you well. The tide became dangerously high two hours before it reached its highest point. The seawall broke and people living in the cottages in Fisherman's Row were drowned, whole families of them. The water was too rough anyhow for the boats to go out, and that's why the men were at home. But the houses further inland were on higher ground. The people fled and were saved. One young boy, whose name was Per, volunteered to ride on his bicycle along the coast road, which was only a rough track, to the tower. It was a lookout post in those days, and a warning could be flashed to neighboring villages. No one knows exactly what happened, but Devil's Dike must have been in flood, and Per was swept away, perhaps while crossing the plank. They found his bicycle long afterwards, but his body was never found, God rest his soul."

"So he never reached the tower?"

"No. He never got there. But the lookout man saw the danger and sent out warning messages."

"So he didn't actually save anybody?"

"It isn't known that he did. And he couldn't save himself. But no brave deed is ever done in vain."

The boys thanked Mr. Penrose and left for home. They could see the lights in the cottage windows and hear the sound of the waves in the darkness, the sound so familiar and yet so haunting, especially at night.

Roger and Sam hoped daily that they might meet

Per again, but as the days grew shorter and the wind off the sea colder, there seemed fewer and fewer chances. When school let out for Christmas, they still had not come across him.

The first few days of the holidays were always the same. The boys felt restless and could not settle to anything. They went on the bus to Queen's Lynn and looked around Woolworth's. They made a few Christmas cards for their parents and grandparents. Roger practiced carols as he was to go carol singing and to take his violin with him unless it rained. Sam started a thorough overhauling of his stamp collection.

On Christmas Eve, Sam suggested that they go watch the excavator that was working near Devil's Bridge. They walked, as the wind made riding almost impossible, even for hardy cyclists like themselves.

It was very satisfying to watch the huge machine opening its steel jaws and grabbing up mouthfuls of marshland.

"Look," said Roger suddenly. "There's something lying beyond the dike that might be an old bicycle."

"Let's go and look."

They crossed the bridge and examined the shapeless tangle of bent iron that might, once, have been a bicycle. Just then the driver of the excavator stopped and lit a cigarette.

"Did you dig up that old bike?" shouted Sam.

"No. I only came on this morning. The chap working yesterday must have found it. If it *is* a bicycle. It looks a right proper mess to me."

"It's a bike, all right. I can see traces of a leather saddle and this crumpled bit was the frame."

"Perhaps you're right. It must have been lying around for many years, buried under the mud. No one'll miss it. No one knew it was there, likely enough."

He prepared to make another grab at the newly deepened dike, and the boys set off for home.

"Do you think it was Per's bike?" said Sam.

"Yes, I do. Mr. Penrose said he was probably drowned somewhere near the bridge. I expect when his bike was found, it was too rusty to be worth repairing. Someone just left it there, and it stayed there till yesterday getting covered with mud."

"Now it's gone forever. Not even a ghost could ride it."

"I don't think we'll ever see Per again," said Roger. "Per and his bicycle seemed to belong together."

"They did. And now he can't ride anymore. He was a marvelous rider. What muscles he had!"

"And what courage! I wonder what he thought about as he raced towards the tower, hearing the waves pounding on the seawall."

"And hearing the roar as they broke through."

"I expect he just thought about getting there, like us when we're racing. We only think about winning the race."

"I shall miss him, in a way," said Sam.

"So shall I. It was exciting always thinking he *might* appear."

"He still might."

"I suppose he just might."

But both boys were sure, as they plodded home with the wind in their faces, that they would never see Per again, with his fair hair and pale face and white clothes. And they never did, except sometimes in dreams, where the dead and the living meet.

The Sunday Child

During the week, when Helen woke up in the morning, she looked at one of her books. She could not read very well yet, but that did not matter. Her father or her mother read to her every night at bedtime, and if she knew the story well enough she could look at the pictures and tell the story over again to Honey, her teddy bear.

Honey listened with his bright glass eyes fixed on the page. He was very good at listening. There was no need to say, "Are you sitting comfortably?" because he was always comfortable and never fidgeted, propped up against the pillow. He never got tired of hearing the same story again and again. He never even yawned.

But Sunday morning was different. Helen loved Sunday mornings. She waited till the clock in her room had its hands at half-past seven, then she arranged Honey nicely with a favorite picture in front of him, perhaps of The Three Bears, and she put on her dressing gown and ran quickly along the landing to her parents' room.

Her father was usually still asleep, but her mother whispered, "Come along, darling, it's cozy in my bed. Do you want something to play with?"

Helen often asked, "May I bring your jewel box?" and her mother always smiled and said, "Yes."

She fetched the jewel box out of a drawer and carried it very carefully, with both hands, to the bed. Then Mother held it while she scrambled into bed beside her.

Helen knew everything in the jewel box by heart. It was made of wood, and lined with red velvet. There was a tray at the top which lifted out and had little partitions for special things in it, and a place for rings. It was big and heavy and full of lovely things. There were jewels that Daddy had given to Mother and things she had had when she was a little girl and other ones that her mother had given her. There were even a few things that had belonged to her grandmother, who was Helen's great-grandmother.

Helen often brought the hand mirror from her mother's dressing table so that she could look at herself while she tried on various necklaces and brooches. She loved the pearl necklace made with three strings of pearls, and the gold locket on a gold chain which opened and showed a tiny picture of herself on one side, and of her father on the other. There were black and white beads from Africa and crystal beads from Italy. There were two strings of coral, one smooth and one made of jagged teeth.

There were bracelets, too, with green emeralds and yellow topazes set in them. They fitted around her mother's wrist, but Helen's arms were so thin that she could push them right up above her elbow.

One Sunday morning, when Helen was exploring the jewel box, she suddenly exclaimed, "There's a new ring here that I've never seen before. It isn't in the proper place with the other rings. Look, a little gold one with a blue stone in it. It's so small it must have been made for someone of my size."

"Oh that," said her mother. "That's very old. It was my mother's when she was a child, and I believe it had been in the family for many years before that. The blue stone is a turquoise."

Helen tried the ring on each of her fingers in turn. It was a perfect fit on her middle finger or the finger next to the little one.

"I wonder why I've never seen it before."

"Well, I haven't seen it for years either. I don't know where it has been unless it had slipped through this tear in the lining. I must mend the tear with something."

Helen put the jewels back in their right places, but kept the ring out. She put it on her finger and lay back and admired it.

"Mother, could I wear this lovely ring? It fits me so nicely and I love it so much."

"Well, dear, I don't like little girls wearing rings. They get in the way and catch in things. And you might lose it."

"But a child wore it once. If I wait till I'm older, it won't go on my finger. I shall have grown too big."

"That's true," said her father, who had just woken up. "It won't fit her for long. Why not let her wear it for a treat?"

"Yes," said Helen, "just for a treat. Just for a Sunday treat."

"All right," said her mother. "Just for a Sunday treat. And you'd better take it off when you go out or play in the garden."

Helen was delighted with her ring. She showed it to Honey who liked it, too. Indeed, he liked it so much that she threaded him a bead bracelet to wear around his paw, as he hadn't any fingers for a ring.

It was pouring rain after breakfast and very cold. Helen said she would go and play in the nursery, which was an attic at the top of the house. She had her dolls' house there, and her rocking horse, and a box of bricks. There were shelves, too, for books and puzzles and other toys.

As soon as she opened the door, she knew there was something different. Perhaps several things. The first one she noticed was that a fire blazed and crackled in the grate. This was strange, as the room was always heated by an electric heater. But there was something else, or rather someone else, who drew her attention. There was a strange girl there, sitting by the window, with some needlework on her lap.

"Who are you?" asked Helen.

"I'm Charity. Who are you?"

"I'm Helen and I live here."

"So do I. Or I think I do."

"Do you like sewing?" asked Helen.

"Not really. Do you?"

"No, I don't, unless Mother makes a sewing card for me. She draws a picture on the card and pricks holes around the edge and then I sew in and out of the holes with a big needle and bright wool. I did a yellow cat the other day."

"That sounds rather babyish. I learned to do cross-stitch when I was four. I'm doing a sampler. I do one letter after breakfast and one after lunch and one after tea. That makes three a day."

"I can hardly see the eye of your needle, it's so tiny," said Helen. "What are the words you are sewing?"

"It's a text from the Bible. It says: 'It's more blessed to give than to receive.' "

"What does that mean?"

"I don't know. There, I have done a 'b.' It will be an 'l' next and that's easy."

"Aren't you bored with all those tiny, tiny black crosses, making all those tiny, tiny black letters?"

"What's 'bored'?"

"Well, kind of fed up."

"What's 'fed up'?"

"Well, tired."

" Oh, yes. I'm tired of them right enough. But when I've finished the letters, which will be in about eight days, I can start on the border. That will be a nice change. It has flowers and leaves and birds and I can use any color in my workbox."

"Pink is my favorite," said Helen.

"Red is mine," said Charity.

She stuck her needle in her work and folded it neatly and put it in the drawer.

"Let's play with your dolls," suggested Helen, seeing several about.

"I don't usually play with them on Sunday," said Charity doubtfully. "I can do my sampler because it's a text from the Bible, and I can do my jigsaw puzzle of *Moses in the Bulrushes*, or look at the pictures in my big Bible. And there's a book I may read called *Sermons for the Young*, but I don't like it much."

"I know I wouldn't like it," said Helen. "I can play with anything I like on Sundays; so can you because we're playing together. We won't do anything noisy or naughty."

"Very well," said Charity. "Let's play with Rosa, my best doll. She was sick in the night."

The two girls knelt down by Rosa's wooden cradle. Rosa was wearing a white nightgown and a little cap.

"I'd better wrap her in a shawl," said Charity, taking a pink fleecy shawl from the cupboard. "She must be kept warm."

"Let's put her close to this roaring fire," suggested Helen. "That would be cozy for her."

She took the cradle in her arms and carried it nearer to the fireguard. Charity gave a cry of horror and snatched the cradle away.

"You must never, never do that. Rosa is made of wax and she'll melt away. Never mind, my precious, you shan't melt away. I will look after you."

She took Rosa in her arms and kissed her pink, waxen cheeks. Then she noticed Helen's ring, and looked at it in a rather puzzled way.

"I believe I had a ring like that once. But I'm not sure. It's very, very pretty. I wish I had a thread as blue as that for my border."

The two girls were kept busy as Rosa took a turn for the worse and the doctor had to be sent for. He advised a cold compress on her chest, and they wrung out a handkerchief in cold water and applied it. This was Charity's idea. They were planning to make some medicine for her, and perhaps some pills, when a voice called up from below, "Helen."

"I must go," said Helen, "but you can come as well. Mother won't mind. She likes me to have someone to play with as I'm an only child."

But suddenly Charity wasn't there. The nursery was just as usual. Helen ran downstairs and sat quietly sipping her fruit juice.

"Penny for your thoughts," said her father, putting his arm around her.

"They're worth more than that. They're worth a hundred pounds."

"Then you can keep them," he laughed.

The next Sunday was fine and sunny, and the whole family went for a walk and picked up acorns. When they got home, Helen put on her ring, and she and her mother made a little acorn man. He had an acorn cup for a hat, a round acorn for a head, a big acorn for a body, and pins for arms and legs. His face was inked in with a marking pen, and he had three ink dots for buttons. They called him Acorn Bill.

"I must show him to Charity," began Helen, and then stopped.

"Does she go to your school?" asked her father. "It's a very old-fashioned name."

"No." Helen shook her head. "She—well, she lives here in the nursery. But I don't think you'll ever see her. She's too shy."

Her father and mother looked at each other and smiled. Helen had often played with pretend companions. For weeks she had carried an imaginary mouse around in her pocket, saving crumbs for it and stroking it. Now she had a child. There was no harm in it if it kept her happy.

After lunch, her father went off to play golf, and her mother said she would have a rest and read her library book.

"I'll go in the nursery," said Helen happily.

"I'll come up later and we'll do something together. Shall I read to you, or shall we play a card game?"

"You needn't come, Mother, really you needn't. I shall be quite all right. Besides, I may have Charity to play with. May I have some more pins, and perhaps she and I can make some acorn people? I've lots of spare acorns."

"Here you are. But don't prick yourselves. Of course, darling, if you do get tired of playing with Charity, give me a call."

Helen flew upstairs and burst into the nursery. She

was very pleased to see that the fire was burning and Charity was doing her sampler by the window.

"I'm just finishing an 'e' in the last word. Tomorrow I'll finish all the letters and on Tuesday I'll start on the border. Oh, how glad I shall be! Flowers and leaves and birds will be so much more interesting."

"Look at Acorn Bill," said Helen. "I've brought lots of acorns and pins so we can make more acorn people."

Charity quickly finished her last letter and folded up her sampler and put it neatly away. Then she and Helen began to play with the acorns.

Charity was very skillful and clever with her fingers. She made an acorn woman and put a paper bonnet on her head, and a paper skirt around her waist. She made a tiny acorn dog with a piece of string for a tail. They both smoked acorn pipes as they worked. When they heard Helen's mother running upstairs. Charity vanished like a dream, leaving her acorn toys behind her.

"This is pretty," said Mother, picking up the acorn woman. "And the dog is a pet. I wish he were mine."

"Charity made them," said Helen proudly. "She's much, much cleverer than me. She can sew, too. She's making a simpler."

"I think you mean a sampler. She must be very clever indeed."

Sunday became the highlight of the week for Helen, and her happiness seemed to begin from the moment she slipped the ring on her finger. She usually had Charity to play with, though she could never be sure about her visits. Sometimes she did not come. When

Helen asked her next time where she had been, she looked worried and a frown came over her face.

"They kept me," or, "I had to learn a psalm and I got it wrong," or once, "I had a fever." But she was usually there, sweet tempered and full of good ideas.

Sometimes they played with Charity's toys. She had a wooden cup and a ball, which was new to Helen. Also some beautifully colored marbles, and some farm animals, each carved by hand. Best of all, there was a nightingale in a golden cage. Charity wound him up and he trilled and chirruped and flapped his wings and nodded his head.

They drew pictures on Charity's slate with a slate pencil. Helen often made the slate pencil squeak horribly when she was drawing.

"Why doesn't it squeak when you're using it?" she said rather crossly.

"Because I'm used to it," said Charity. "I learned to write my ABCs and my numbers on a slate. I used to make squeaks when I began. I don't now."

One Sunday, Helen ran up to the nursery and found it was a day when Charity was not there. She walked around the room, touching things and opening and shutting books. Nothing was tempting to play with. She particularly wanted Charity that day as she thought they might play at dressing up. There was a box full of dressing-up clothes in the cupboard just for that purpose. Then, as she opened the cupboard door to rummage in the box, she saw her hand on the knob, plain and bare without her Sunday ring. She ran off to fetch it from her handkerchief drawer where it was kept, slipped it on her finger, and ran back upstairs. She felt sure that all would be well this time, and it was.

The fire was blazing, and Charity was sitting peacefully working at her sampler. She was doing the colored border now.

"Hurry up, Charity. Let's dress up. I've got lots of dressing-up clothes."

"And so have I. But I must just finish a petal of this flower first."

Helen watched Charity's needle flashing in and out, making the red petal. She wore a silver thimble with her name engraved inside. When the petal was done, she folded her work away in the drawer.

Charity opened the cupboard and got out, not Helen's carton of clothes, but a basket with a double lid that Helen had never seen before. Soon the girls were absorbed in trying on. They took off their dresses first, and Helen saw that Charity was wearing two petticoats, a flannel one and a white one. Also long white panties with lace around the bottom. She called these her "drawers."

They hobbled about in high-heeled satin slippers much too big for them, and trailed long, flowing, flowery dresses and black skirts on the floor. Helen fell in love with a little white fur muff with a cord to hang around her neck.

Charity was still fascinated by the ring on Helen's finger. She was always saying how pretty it was.

"I know I had a ring just like that once," she said. "But I don't seem to have it now."

She was very pleased when Helen let her wear it for a few minutes. She kept touching it and turning her hand this way and that so the light glinted on the blue stone.

"It's a turquoise," said Helen.

"I know," replied Charity. "Mama told me."

The Sunday before Christmas Helen ran up to the nursery and found Charity in tears. She was crying so much that at first she could not say what was wrong. She just held Helen's hand tightly and sobbed.

"Let me fetch Mother," begged Helen. "She's so good at comforting people, much better than me. She's the best person in the world."

But Charity shook her head.

At last Helen could make out the words that Charity was struggling to say. Her little striped cat Tibby was dead. He had come in from the garden and refused all food and crept into his basket and died.

Helen did not know what to say. She could only squeeze Charity's hand and repeat over and over again, "I'm so sorry. I'm so sorry. I'm so very, very sorry."

It would be no good saying, "Maybe you can have another cat," because she knew Charity only wanted her own dear Tibby. Then she had a wonderful idea which came like a flash.

"Charity, you can have my ring, you know, the one you like so much. The one like the ring you once had. Here it is. It's yours. Put it on."

She slipped the ring off her finger and held it out.

Charity smiled through her tears and put it on. Gradually she stopped crying, though her breath still came in gasps.

"Thank you very much. It's very, very kind of you. Can you really spare it?"

"Of course I can. It's yours for keeps."

They spent the rest of the time playing with the dolls' tea set, made of thin china with tiny roses on it. A nice cup of sugar-and-water tea did them both good.

The next Sunday was Christmas Day. Helen didn't have a moment to spare all day. There was her stocking to unpack and her presents to open. Her best present was a new bicycle and she spent most of the morning riding around and around the garden. Then friends came to tea and afterwards the Christmas tree was lit up and there were more presents and games.

When she was having her bath, rather later than usual, her mother suddenly said, "Where is your ring?"

Then Helen remembered about Charity and how she had completely forgotten her all day. She burst into tears. Mother thought she was crying because she had lost the ring.

"Never mind, darling. We'll almost certainly find it somewhere in the house or garden. You'd soon have outgrown it, anyhow. Don't cry on Christmas Day."

"We won't find it, ever. I've given it to Charity, and I can't ask for it back again. She loves it so."

Mother tucked her in bed and Daddy read a very comforting story about the little elves who helped a poor shoemaker.

When the next Sunday came, it began as usual, with

Helen going into Mother's bed at half-past seven. After breakfast she ran upstairs to the nursery, but even as she put her hand on the knob of the door she felt that the room was empty.

There was no coal fire and no Charity. The room was warm from the heater, but it felt forsaken and un-friendly. She tried again, many times, during the day, and called Charity's name again and again. But there was no answer. She felt that there would never be an answer.

It's just as though she needed the ring, thought Helen. She always wanted it. And it wasn't really mine.

Soon she did not miss Charity so badly, especially when her own cat, Willow, had a family of kittens, and she sat next to a new friend at school, called Jennifer. But she never forgot Charity. Sundays were never the same without her.

"Mother," she said one Sunday morning, when they were in bed together. "Will you tell me what something means? What does it mean to say, 'It is more blessed to give than to receive?' "

"It means that it's better to give something away than to have something given to you. Especially if it's something the other person really needs."

"I see," said Helen.

There was a pause, then she said cheerfully, "Mother, may I look at your jewel box? I haven't been through it for ages."

Cherry Ripe

Giles had been ill. First he had been in the hospital, in a ward with a shiny red floor, two rows of beds, and jars of flowers on a long table. Then he had gone home to lie in his own bed in his own room, with his books on the shelves and his toys in the cupboard. Now he was well enough to get up and dress, and sit in a chair in the living room, while his little sisters, aged two and four, played about on the floor and drew pictures for him.

Giles and the rest of the family lived in a flat in London. It was up a great many stairs, and until his legs got strong again he could not walk up and down them.

"Soon you will need a holiday," said his mother. "You must go to the seaside or into the country where you can have plenty of fresh air."

"You'll come, too, won't you?" asked Giles anxiously.

"We'll see," said his mother, and Giles felt that this meant he was to go away without her.

"I don't care much for vacations," he said. "I like home best. I like being just like this, with the girls playing about and Father coming home in the evening and you always here. Can you read to me now?"

Then, if his mother wasn't too busy, she would sit down and read *Swiss Family Robinson* till it was time to get another meal.

Giles was quite content to lie on the sofa and hear his mother's voice going on and on, clearly and gently.

When it was time for his medicine, the little girls came to watch him swallow the stuff and to smell the bottle. When he had a chocolate drop to take the taste away, they had one too.

One morning a letter came which both Father and Mother read several times.

"A good idea. Excellent!" said his father, as he went off to work. "Fix it up as soon as you can."

"What is a good idea?" asked Giles. "What are you going to fix up? Is it something about me?"

"Yes, it is," said his mother, coming and sitting on his bed, the letter in her hand. "It is a letter from your Great Aunt Flo."

"What is a great aunt? Do I know her? What does she want?"

"She is really my aunt Flo, and my aunts are your great aunts. She lives in the country with a garden nearly as big as a park and has invited you to stay with her. You could be out-of-doors almost all day long, and you'd get well twice as quickly if you went. Why, you might be able to play cricket this summer, and swim, and do all the nice things we do when we go to the sea-side in August."

"Could I climb trees?"

"I think you could soon."

"And if I don't like it, may I come home?"

"Why, yes."

"Then I'll go and see if I like it."

By the time Giles's suitcase was packed, he was looking forward to going away. Every time one of his sisters said, "I wish I was coming," he felt glad it was he who was going, His father came in the train with him as far as Ipswich. There he put Giles into a slow local train that would take him to Great Aunt Flo's village.

"It's the sixth stop," said his father. "Don't lose your ticket."

"No, I won't," said Giles cheerfully. "Good-bye!"

Giles expected Great Aunt Flo to be very old indeed. Perhaps she would meet him with a horse and buggy like Mr. McGregor in *Peter Rabbit*. Perhaps she was deaf. Perhaps she walked with a cane. When he arrived at the sixth stop, he recognized her at once, as soon as he got out of the train. As she was the only lady on the platform, it wasn't difficult.

She had white hair, it was true, but she walked quickly with long strides and picked up his suitcase as if it weighed nothing at all. A gray Bentley car was parked outside, and they were soon driving down a winding country lane, with hedges on each side and green fields beyond. Giles kept seeing streams he would like to paddle in and boughs he would like to swing from.

They went up a drive and stopped in front of a red brick house. It had rows and rows of windows and very tall chimneys. There were steps up to the front door, which had a heavy brass knocker. When Giles had washed his hands, he found Great Aunt Flo in the drawing room with the tea beside her on a cart. The bread and butter was very thin and there was no cake.

"Go into the kitchen and have tea with Mrs. Best," she said. "She'll take care of you. She's brought up ten children of her own, five boys and five girls, so you'll be all right with her."

Giles went thankfully into the kitchen. Until that moment, he was not sure whether he liked staying with Great Aunt Flo, and he wondered how soon he could ask his mother if he could go home. But tea with Mrs. Best put his mind at rest. She welcomed him as if she had known him all his life.

"Come along, Giles. I've boiled you an egg and here's a plate of banana sandwiches. You'll soon get better if you eat well and sleep well."

"Will you tell me about your ten children, especially the naughty ones?" asked Giles, taking the top off his egg, and helping himself to a thickly buttered crust.

"Of course I will," said Mrs. Best. While Giles ate his egg and the sandwiches and drank his milk, she told him about her five girls with long, fair pigtails, and the five boys who used to tie their sisters' pigtails to the backs of their chairs, and then run away and leave them. Before he had heard half enough, he had eaten an enormous meal and, as Mrs. Best said, looked fatter already.

There was a box in the corner of the kitchen with a cat and four kittens inside.

"You can choose one for yourself, if you like," said Mrs. Best. "I expect your mother will let you take one home. They'll be old enough to leave their mother by then."

Giles spent the time before going to bed kneeling beside the box, playing with the kittens, and trying to decide which was the prettiest. When Mrs. Best said, "Time for bed," he had just decided on the black one with the white paws and the white bib under his chin.

Before they left the kitchen, Mrs. Best measured Giles against the door. She made a thick black mark with her pencil and wrote his initials and the date below it. "You'll be taller as well as heavier when you leave," she said.

His bedroom was very large, larger than any of the rooms at home. There was a mirror on the dressing table and he did not like a strange yellow glow in one corner of it. He quickly looked away. The bed was high and wide. He seemed to sink into it so that he hardly made a mound under the bedclothes. The quilt looked flat. He hastily stuck up his toes and was relieved to see two peaks rising.

"Are you comfortable?" asked Mrs. Best, tucking him in.

"Yes," replied Giles doubtfully. "Yes."

"I'll leave the door ajar and if you want anything, just call or knock on the wall at the head of your bed. My room is next door."

"Oh, thank you," smiled Giles. "But I don't suppose I shall want anything. I never do, you know."

Now that he was near to Mrs. Best, the room seemed smaller. The curtains appeared less thick and dark. The queer light in the looking glass wasn't frightening—it was just the reflection of the brass knobs on the bedstead.

Giles began to choose names for the kitten. Whitefoot. Whitepaw. Paddy. He had only thought of three when he was fast asleep.

The next day he woke with a start and felt, at once, that everything was different. Of course the bed and the furniture and the curtains were different, that was to be expected, but he seemed to be in a different world. There was no rumble and roar of buses and cars and not even the noise of his mother busy in the flat, clinking china and shutting doors. The kitchen was so far away that even if Mrs. Best were smashing cups or slamming doors, Giles would never hear a sound.

Outside there was only the crowing of a cock, the occasional barking of a dog, and the distant hum of what might be an airplane. It was a tractor, but Giles did not know it. He got out of bed and dressed and went towards the stairs.

The walls of the corridors and the staircase were hung with portraits in dingy gilt frames. They were all of old people in old-fashioned clothes. Their favorite colors seemed to be brown and purple and black, and he did not feel tempted to stop and look more closely. So many large, severe faces, with white hair and beaked noses, were best passed by with a glance. But halfway downstairs there was a small landing, and here hung the portrait of a child.

Giles stood still and looked with pleasure at the girl in her long white frock with a red sash and a bunch of red cherries in one hand. She had dark curls and dark eyes and a mischievous expression. Her lips were parted, perhaps because she was going to burst out laughing, or perhaps pop in another cherry.

The artist had painted the girl sitting down, but she appeared ready to jump up at any moment and run off. Giles went on downstairs, determined to come back often and look at the lively little cherry girl. She seemed out of place among all the elderly ladies and gentlemen, as he felt out of place in this large, silent house.

He had a game with Whitepaw, though Whitepaw was too young to do much except bite a finger with lovely little white teeth like ivory needles. His claws, when he clung to the front of Giles's sweater, were no bigger than rose thorns. But they were sharp and curved. The front of the sweater was soon covered with tufts of wool that these tiny claws had pulled out.

Breakfast was a cheerful meal in Mrs. Best's sunny kitchen. When he had eaten all he wanted and left the table, there was nothing else he really wanted to do. He wandered about the garden, along gravel paths and over smooth lawns, past flower beds and vegetable plots. But there was nothing to do to pass the time. The trees did not look the kind for children to climb, and the lawns were useless without a ball or someone else to play with.

During the morning the doctor came. He looked as old as the portraits on the walls, but he was gentle and friendly. He asked Giles a few questions, listened to his chest, and told Great Aunt Flo to see that he had plenty of food, fresh air, and sleep.

"Two Fs and an S," he said. "You'll be fit as a fiddle in a few weeks."

"What can I *do?*" asked Giles despairingly. "What can I *do?*"

"Ah, you're missing your sisters," said the doctor. "Well, if someone mends the old swing, you could play on that. Will that do for a start?"

"Oh, yes," said Giles. "It will do beautifully. I've never had a swing of my own. I've only played on the ones in the park with chains instead of ropes, and I always get splinters in my hands off the rough seats. I would like to swing very, very much."

After lunch, Mrs. Best suggested that he might like to write to his family. He sat down at once with the paper and pencil he had brought from home. Mrs. Best sharpened the pencil twice and helped him with the spelling.

When the letter was finished, the gardener put his head around the door and said the swing was now mended. Mrs. Best addressed the envelope for Giles, and he hurried out to the paddock, a small enclosed field where the swing hung from the bough of a tree. It was only a wooden seat with brand new ropes attached, but the seat was polished smooth as if a great many children had played on it. The ropes were threaded through holes in the seat, and underneath each was tied in a big knot so it could not slip through.

Soon Giles was swinging gently to and fro, pushing off the ground with his feet. Then, when he got going, he found he could work himself higher and higher by bending backwards and forwards. He soon got hot and tired and had to stop for a rest, but the rests grew fewer and shorter and he found he could swing higher and higher. It was tea-time before he even began to feel hungry, the afternoon had passed so quickly.

The next few days seemed long ones in spite of the swing. Every day he wrote to his family, and every day he looked at the girl with the cherries as he went up and down the stairs. Every day, almost, he asked Mrs. Best to measure him again to see if he had grown, but she repeated that if he had, it was too little to measure.

Whitepaw grew bigger and could walk on the kitchen floor. He tried to follow the end of a piece of string which Giles dragged along, but he soon got tired and scrambled back into the box with his mother and the other kittens.

The swing was still the best plaything of all. Often Giles did not bother to go really high, but just sat there in the sun, holding the ropes loosely, and dreaming. Once, when he ran to the paddock, he found the swing was gently moving. When he sat on it, the seat felt warm. It was as if someone had been swinging on it and had run away when they saw him coming. But of course it was warm from the sun, thought Giles, and the wind might have blown it. Only it was a calm, dull day, so they were not very suitable explanations.

Another time, when he had invented a jumping-off game, he had the same feeling that he was not alone. When he had worked himself up to a good height, he let go of the ropes and jumped off into the long grass. After an especially high jump he was sure someone nearby gave an "O-o-oh!" of surprise.

Then, when he had been playing by himself for two weeks, he actually saw another child in the garden, sitting on the swing. It was a girl about his own age. He was pleased to see her, but not so pleased to see her playing on his swing.

"Why aren't you at school?" asked Giles.

"Why aren't you?" replied the girl.

"I've been ill and I'm getting better."

"I'm getting better, too," said the girl, though her cheeks were so rosy that it was difficult to imagine her ever having been ill.

"I'm staying here," said Giles. "Where do you live?"

"Very near. I'm almost at home," and she laughed.

"Does your mother know my Great Aunt Flo?"

"I expect so. She knows most of the people around here."

Giles gave up asking questions because the little girl only put him off with her answers, and seemed to be making fun of him.

"I'll show you how to do a twizzle on your swing," said the little girl, "only it might make you feel ill. It nearly makes me feel ill when I'm quite well."

"I'm quite well enough to do a twizzle," said Giles. "Quite. Please show me."

"Sit still on the swing and hold tight."

She turned Giles and the swing around and around and around till the two ropes were twisted together as if they were one thick rope.

"Now I'm going to un-twizzle you."

She spun him in the opposite direction and Giles whizzed around and around till he felt sick and dizzy, as the ropes untwisted. Then he turned slower and slower till he was back where he had started.

"Shall I give you one?" he suggested, when the ground had stopped going around.

"Yes, please."

"Tighter—tighter—turn me around once more, just once more!" said the girl, as Giles wound up the twizzle.

"Now let me go."

When the spinning was over and the ropes straight once more, her cheeks were redder than ever.

"Let's play hide-and-seek," she said. "I know all the good places."

"Yes, but—" began Giles. "But I'm only supposed to play quiet games till I'm quite well. Of course I'm nearly well now, more than three-quarters."

"We'll leave hide-and-seek till later on," the girl agreed cheerfully. "I'm only supposed to play quiet games, too."

"Because you've been ill?"

"Partly. And partly because of getting dirty and untidy. They want me to grow up into a lady."

"You'll do that anyhow," said Giles seriously. "You can't expect to grow up into a man."

"Oh, not just that kind of a lady," laughed the girl. "I don't mind that. I don't want to be a man and have to go to the wars. No, they just mean a fine lady. A grand lady. Someone who likes pretty clothes and has the vapors and doesn't romp about."

"What are 'the vapors'?" asked Giles.

"I haven't the least idea, but I don't like the sound of them, do you? I've made up my mind never to have them. And I shall romp as much as I like!"

"You said once you'd been ill, too."

"So I did. I was ill, I remember. The doctor was there and my father and mother and the priest. But I can't remember what happened next. They put a spoonful of something horrid between my lips. I tried to spit it out. I remember trying." She looked so worried that Giles felt sorry for her.

"Never mind what happened next," he said "I expect you went to sleep. I kept falling asleep when I was ill. Then you must have waked up much better or you wouldn't be here, would you?"

"No, I wouldn't." She looked much happier. "I must have gotten better without knowing it." And she jumped up and turned a lightning somersault in spite of her long dress.

"Bother my dress! It gets in the way terribly. I wish

I were dressed like you." She looked enviously at Giles's gray shorts and blue sweater.

"But lots of girls wear shorts. Even my sisters who are only two and four wear them sometimes. Haven't you any clothes beside that party dress?"

She looked worried again. "I used to. But I'm not sure where they are. I don't think I could find them now."

"Let's go to the thicket and gather fir cones," said Giles. "That's quiet."

"Yes, let's. Where shall we put them?"

"In the hollow tree. They'll keep dry there. One day we can have a bonfire of them and roast potatoes in the hot ashes. I've read in books of children doing that, but I've never done it myself."

"That would be lovely. The best thing I've ever done in my life."

The thicket was a little wood, and they collected fir cones from under the fir trees and stowed them neatly inside the hollow trunk of an oak. Considering that it was supposed to be a quiet game, they got surprisingly hot and dirty.

Then the gong sounded for Giles's dinner.

"See you tomorrow," said Giles, as he stuffed a last handful of cones in its place.

"Yes, see you tomorrow."

"What's your name? Mine's Giles."

"Mine's Caroline."

"Good-bye, Caroline."

"Good-bye, Giles."

Giles said nothing about Caroline as he ate his dinner. He wasn't sure if she ought to be in the garden at all. He was certain that Great Aunt Flo didn't know about her. Where could she live? There were no other houses near, except a cottage or two, dotted about. Yet she had said, "I'm almost at home."

He stopped wondering and ate an extra large meal.

"Do, please, measure me again," he begged Mrs. Best. "I feel so tall tonight. I'm sure I've grown."

So Mrs. Best measured him carefully against the door and drew another line with her pencil. Yes, he had grown.

"An eighth of an inch!" said Mrs. Best proudly, as if it were she who had grown.

Whitepaw seemed to have grown, too. That evening, he found he could pounce. He crouched down, even flattening his tiny ears. When Giles pulled the string past, he jumped up in the air and tried to bite it.

"Oh, you fierce tiger cat!" said Giles.

Whitepaw smiled and showed his pink gums and his white teeth. Then the smile changed into a yawn and he scrambled back into the box, mewing and struggling when his mother seized him and began to wash him. She washed the kittens many times a day, however much they cried.

When Giles went up to bed, he stopped, as usual, on the little landing where the portrait of the girl in white hung. She seemed livelier than ever.

It's the best picture in the whole house, he thought to himself. I should think it is the best in the whole world. She looks so alive. I like her better than anyone here, except Mrs. Best and Whitepaw.

The next day was sunny and warm, and Giles met Caroline by the swing. They had swings in turn, and gave each other twizzles. Then they began to make a house for themselves in the thicket. They used dead branches and dead ferns from the ditch. The floor was laid with moss. This was the longest job of all till they found a mossy stretch of stone wall. The floor, when finished, was soft enough, but rather wet.

Caroline took her sash off and tied it over the doorway.

"It's the House of the Red Banner," she said.

They played in the house again in the afternoon, making all kinds of improvements. They built a fireplace of stones, and a little storehouse of old bricks, though they had nothing to store in it. They found a stone with a deep hollow in it which they filled with water from the lily pond, and floated tulip petals in it. Caroline was most particular that there should not be two petals alike.

When the gong sounded for tea, Caroline could not untie her sash.

"Help me," she cried. "Help me, Giles."

They both tugged and pulled, but the knots only got tighter. Giles tried his teeth, but the knots got wet and slippery and even more difficult. Then the gong sounded again, for the second time.

"Never mind. You must go," said Caroline. "And so must I. Good-bye, Giles."

"Good-bye, Caroline. See you tomorrow. Never mind about the sash."

"Oh, *I* don't mind, but *they* may," said Caroline sadly. "They are always minding about something or other."

That night, as Giles went up to bed, he gazed for a long time at the portrait. It looked different. The girl's face was the same, rosy and smiling, and the cherries were red and juicy, but something was different.

"She hasn't her sash on," said Giles to himself. "She's lost her sash. So she couldn't untie it after all."

Whatever am I thinking? Why did I say that? But I've always known the portrait was Caroline, though I've never properly thought about it. It's her face and smile and white dress and black slippers and everything. So of course if Caroline has lost her sash, the girl in the portrait has lost hers, too. I don't understand. I just know.

Mrs. Best came upstairs to wash his hair, but he did not mention the lost sash to her. As she rubbed his hair dry, exclaiming at all the bits of twig and dirt that had come out, he began to wonder if the picture had had a sash. Perhaps the red he remembered was the red of the cherries and the red of Caroline's lips? It didn't really matter. He would see Caroline tomorrow and he could ask about the sash.

The next day, as the two of them played by their house in the thicket with the red sash waving over the door, Giles said casually, "There's a picture of you halfway up the stairs. A jolly nice one, too."

"Yes, I remember sitting for it. Oh, how tired and stiff I used to get. Oh, the pins and needles in my feet and the ache in my neck! And the cherries were so tempting. I sometimes managed to eat one when no one was looking."

"But that must have been ages ago," said Giles. "The picture is old, I'm sure. It must have been painted before I was born."

Caroline's face clouded. She seemed ready to cry. Her lips trembled.

"It couldn't be," she said. "It was only last summer. It was before I had the smallpox. It was when the cherries were ripe on the orchard wall. It couldn't have been ages ago! Giles, please don't frighten me. Please don't frighten me!"

She clutched his hand, and he squeezed her cold fingers and said comfortingly, "No, it couldn't have been long ago, and it just doesn't matter. Here we are, the two of us, so let's have fun. Let's do something different. Let's look for an old sack in the stable and see if we can find enough hen feathers and duck feathers to stuff for a pillow. We can sit on it in our house. The moss is so clammy."

This idea took the rest of the day to carry out, though the feathers they found in the hen house and the duck house were not really the kind for a feather pillow. But they filled any spaces with pine needles, and the pillow was certainly large and fat and firm, though not exactly soft.

Caroline rubbed against a post in the hen run and

it left a brown stain on her dress. They wrung it out in the pond and scrubbed it with grass, but the stain only spread into a dark smudge. So they gave up trying. Caroline, as usual, was rather upset as to what "they" would say, but she soon seemed to forget and ran off cheerfully when the tea gong sounded.

As Giles went up to bed, he was not in the least surprised to see a dark stain on the white dress in the portrait. He would have been more surprised if it hadn't been there.

When Mrs. Best came up to say good night, he nearly told her about Caroline, but she seemed so slow to understand that he soon gave up the attempt.

"Can pictures of people come alive?" he asked.

"No. They can be paintings of living people, that's all."

"I don't mean that. Can a picture ever be alive or move or speak?"

"Only if it's on the films. It can only move otherwise if someone takes it off the wall and carries it."

"Could a picture have a—a kind of ghost?"

"Now we won't talk of ghosts at bedtime," said Mrs. Best brightly. "We don't think of things like that. And ghosts are only made up. Just nonsense. Just poppycock."

"Good night, Mrs. Best," said Giles sadly. It was no use asking her important questions. She didn't even know what they meant.

The days went by quickly, now. Whitepaw could climb up the kitchen curtains when Mrs. Best wasn't looking, and he liked to play in the garden, though a sudden puff of wind would send him scampering towards the back door and safety. He could scratch soil and pretend to sharpen his claws on the trunks of the trees. One day, Giles took him to see Caroline.

"What a darling!" said Caroline, putting out her hand. "Puss! Puss! Come here."

But Whitepaw wouldn't go near, not even when Caroline drew a blade of grass along the ground. He pranced away sideways, his fur standing on end, his eyes dark and wild with fear.

"He isn't very used to girls," explained Giles. "Never mind."

"He doesn't like me," said Caroline sadly. "He's scared. Take him back to his mother."

So Giles took Whitepaw back into the kitchen and his fur lay flat again as he purred with relief.

Giles and Caroline grew more daring and played in the drive, and near the gate and the back door, or within sight of the windows. But though the tradesmen and Mrs. Best waved to Giles when they saw him, or even stopped to talk, no one took any notice of Caroline. No one asked her her name, or what she was doing in the garden. But Caroline could see *them* well enough, and often made comments on the way they dressed or spoke or behaved.

Giles wanted to coax her indoors to see his bedroom, but she only shook her head and said, "I'm better in the open air. I only go indoors when I have to, when they call me. Don't ask me again."

Once Giles went indoors to fetch something and he noticed that the portrait on the stairs was empty. Or rather the frame was still there, and the background of trees and flowers, but there was a space where Caroline should have been in her white dress. He was surprised that no one else had noticed and asked questions.

Gradually, an idea formed in Giles's mind. At first he pushed it aside as being unkind and dangerous, but it kept coming back. He did his best to think of other things, to count from a hundred backwards, and to say poetry, but the idea crept back. When he had got to ten, nine, eight, seven, six, five, four, three, two, one, it was there again. Or when he had finished *This Is the House that Jack Built*, it was worrying him like someone knocking at a door who would not go away.

At last he persuaded himself that it was a joke and that no harm could come. Or if it did, he could easily put things right again. So one afternoon, when Caroline was making daisy chains in the garden, he hurried indoors, stood on a bedroom chair, and lifted the picture off the wall. It was very heavy. He could only just carry it. But he managed to push it onto the window seat in his bedroom, behind one of the heavy velvet curtains. Then he ran back into the garden.

Caroline was pleased with herself as she had a daisy chain on her head, another around her neck, daisy bracelets around each wrist, and she was busy making two anklets.

Giles felt uneasy about his plan, and he was especially nice to Caroline, fastening up the anklets for her, and even allowing her to make him a crown as well, though he had no wish to wear flowers in his hair. When the gong sounded, he lingered by her side, till she said impatiently, "You'd better go before Mrs. Best gets cross."

"I—I didn't hear the gong," lied Giles. "Or I'm not sure that I did. Come indoors with me and I'll show you something interesting."

"Tell me, instead. You know I can't come in."

"I can't tell you. I can only show you. Please come." He took her hand, but she pulled it away.

"Don't bother me. I can't come. And you could tell me if you wanted to."

Just then, the gong sounded louder than before. Giles knew he must go. There was no hope of getting Caroline indoors and showing her where her picture was hidden.

"See you tomorrow, Caroline."

"Yes. Good-bye, Giles."

Giles ate his supper and Great Aunt Flo read to him afterwards in the drawing room. She let him play with Whitepaw while she was reading. Whitepaw did not like being read to, but Giles let him bite the corner of his handkerchief, and soon he fell asleep. Then Mrs. Best fetched him to go to bed.

Giles felt unhappy and unsettled, but at the same time excited. What would Caroline do? Would she find the picture hidden behind the curtain? If not, might she just turn into an ordinary girl? She might even be persuaded to come back to London with him. Or would Great Aunt Flo adopt her? Whatever happened, it would be fun to find out.

When Mrs. Best had tucked him in, he slipped out of bed and peered behind the curtain. The frame was still empty. He meant to stay awake all night, watching and listening, in case Caroline wanted any help in getting back, but he fell asleep at last. When Giles woke, it was pitch dark. He heard someone crying bitterly in the darkness. He got out of bed but could not, at once, find the switch for the light. He felt frightened as he drew his fingers along the wall. Where had the switch gone to? Then his hand found the corner of the room, but still no switch. He could bear it no longer. He thumped on the wall and shouted, "Mrs. Best! Mrs. Best! Mrs. Best!"

"I'm coming, Giles. Just a minute." He heard the click of her light and waited while she scrambled into her dressing gown and slippers. A moment later he was in her arms.

"What are you crying for, my dear? What's breaking your heart? Have you a pain? Is it a bad dream?"

"No. I was wide awake. But I heard someone crying. Listen!"

They both listened, but there was nothing to hear.

"She's quiet now. She isn't crying anymore."

"It wasn't anyone outside," said Mrs. Best. "It was you yourself. I heard you crying when you called me. There's no one here except you and me."

"We must put it back at once," said Giles. "This very minute. We may be too late. Will you help me?"

Mrs. Best had no idea what he meant, but she followed him to the window seat and helped him to pick up the heavy picture.

"We must put it back where it belongs, on the landing halfway downstairs," said Giles. "That was the trouble. I moved it and she couldn't get back. She couldn't find the way."

"I think you are still dreaming," said Mrs. Best gently, "but of course we'll put it back. I think you must have moved the picture in your sleep. You couldn't have carried such a heavy thing by yourself if you'd been awake."

They hung the picture on its hook. Then Mrs. Best tucked him in bed, gave him a drink of water and a pill to swallow, and left his door open. He half knew, half dreamed, that she came to visit him many times in the night, shading her flashlight with her hand.

Next morning, Giles was treated as if he had had a temperature. He had breakfast in bed and wore his robe when he sat up. However, while Mrs. Best was preparing his tray, he tiptoed downstairs and looked at the portrait. Caroline was in her usual place, the red of her lips and cheeks matching the red of the cherries. So all was well. She was safely back where she belonged.

Great Aunt Flo came to see him next, and there was a discussion as to whether the doctor should be called.

"I'm quite well," said Giles. "I've never felt better."

"Do you remember having a bad dream?" asked Mrs. Best.

"I remember something, and you came and gave me a pill."

"Do you ever walk in your sleep at home?" asked Great Aunt Flo.

"No. Why should I? Do people do that?"

The two women talked in whispers, and it was decided not to call the doctor.

"Just have a quiet day," said Mrs. Best. "You must be tired after such a disturbed night."

"I'll read a book on the swing," said Giles, eager to get up, and knowing that Caroline always came to the swing first.

"Very well. But don't get too hot, swinging too high. You must be quite well when you go home in two weeks."

This was the first time Giles had heard that he was to go home so soon, and he longed to tell Caroline and make the most of the time that was left. How terribly he would miss her! And she would miss him more because she hadn't two little sisters to play with. He walked while he was in sight of the windows, and then ran to the swing as fast as he could.

But Caroline was not there. He could hardly believe his eyes. She was always there first, and he was later than usual. He called her name, but there was no answer. He looked in all her favorite places—the house in the thicket, the lily pond, the hollow tree, the bushes in the drive. But there was no sign of her. Once he thought he caught a glimpse of her white dress between green leaves, but it was only the opening flowers of the white lilac.

"Caroline! Caroline!" he called. "Where are you? Don't be angry about last night. Let's make a fire of our pine cones and roast some potatoes. You can light it, I've got a whole box of matches."

Surely that would bring her. But no, the garden stayed empty and silent.

He went indoors and looked at the portrait. Caroline was there smiling, with her red sash tied properly.

He ran back to their house in the thicket. Yes, the red sash had gone from above the door. Perhaps "they" had come and untied it.

The rest of the day seemed endless. There were so many things the two of them could have done, but he didn't have the heart to do any of them alone. He was glad when it was bedtime.

While Mrs. Best was running the bath water and out of sight, he whispered urgently to Caroline, "Please, please come back, if only for once. I'm going home soon and we must say good-bye. I've a present to give you, a surprise." He knew she loved surprises.

Did she nod her head? Did her lips form the word "Yes?" He couldn't be certain. But at least she hadn't looked cross. Surely, surely she would come.

The next morning he was by the swing directly after

breakfast, with the surprise in his hand. It was a small penknife that his father had given him. He knew Caroline would love it, though she might have to keep it hidden from "them." But Caroline was not there. The swing was not moving. There was a film of dew on the seat and it felt cold. At that moment he gave up hope. He knew he would never see Caroline again. She had gone back to wherever she had come from, and he couldn't follow. He knew it was his own fault for trying to bring her into his own world to live. She could only live where she belonged, and he must live where he belonged, without her.

The next week was not so bad after all. He was quite well now and was allowed to go to the farm and feed the chickens and ride on the tractor. He grew another eighth of an inch. He got fatter, too, and Mrs. Best had to move several buttons on his clothes. The doctor said he could go back to school at half-term, and play cricket, and go swimming.

On his last evening, Mrs. Best and he got a basket ready for Whitepaw when he traveled in the train. It had a lid and a soft piece of blanket on the bottom. There was room for Whitepaw to turn around and stretch and curl up. But he couldn't spring out as the lid fastened with a wooden peg.

Then Giles sat with Great Aunt Flo in the drawing room.

"I'm not used to children," said Great Aunt **Flo**, "but I must say you have been a very good boy. **You've** found things to amuse yourself, and you've been no trouble at all. I shall miss you. I hope you'll come again and bring your little sisters."

"I'd love to," said Giles.

"I want to give you a present to take home. Is there anything that has taken your fancy? Something out of the china cabinet, perhaps? This house is so full of things."

Giles blushed and fidgeted. There *was* something, but he didn't like to ask. He felt suddenly shy.

"Go on, speak up!" said Great Aunt Flo impatiently.

"There is something I'd like," confessed Giles. "But I can't possibly ask. You see it's big and valuable. And it's not meant for children."

"Never mind. Out with it. If it's big, I may be very glad indeed to get rid of it. Heaven knows this place is as crowded as a museum. After all, at the worst I can only say no."

Giles took a deep breath and spoke quickly. "It's the portrait of the girl in white, halfway upstairs."

"Oh," said Great Aunt Flo, "you can have that with pleasure. It was done by some unknown painter and is of no special value. I don't know what your parents will say, as it's rather large for a small flat. But of course you can have it. I'll get it packed up properly and sent off by rail."

"Who is the girl?" asked Giles.

"Lady Caroline Peel. She died of smallpox, poor child, over a hundred years ago. She used to live here."

When the portrait arrived at the flat and was hung in Giles's bedroom, it took up most of the wall space over his bed. At first he felt shy with Caroline so near, but he soon got used to her. It was like sharing the room with a friend.

When Giles lifted up Whitepaw to look at Caroline, the cat was not in the least frightened. He just stared with wide blue eyes that were fast turning green. Whitepaw liked Caroline best when she was safe in her frame.

The Whistling Boy

Simon was ten when his family moved from a busy northern city to a little town by the sea. Life changed in one day, but it took more than one day for Simon to get used to the change. It took many days, and indeed many weeks, before he felt really at home in the new surroundings.

In the city, he had lived in a flat in a big block, up on the fifth floor, and there were five more floors above him. The road below was always busy, day and night. Trucks and vans and cars roared by, and the pavements were crowded.

There was nowhere he could ride his new bicycle except on a concrete strip at one side of the block. The nearest park was a bus ride away and when he went there, his mother always impressed on him not to talk to strangers, and not to do anything the keeper wouldn't like, and to be sure to be home before it was dark.

His address used to be: *Flat 6, Floor 5, Tower Block*. Now it was just *Wave Crest, Mill Lane*, and he could see the waves, or at least their white crests, from his bedroom window.

At last he was free to go for walks and bicycle rides, and to play ball on the beach at low tide or on the town green. But at first he could not enjoy all this wonderful freedom to go where he liked, or to do what he liked, because he knew no one to do things with.

There were two weeks before his new school opened. In that time he collected shells and seaweed from the beach, and he cycled around and around the town. He threw hundreds of stones into the sea, and sent postcards to his friends in the flats.

The thing Simon liked best of all, except for the sea itself, was the old castle. It was very old, hundreds of years old, his father said, and it stood on the cliffs. Part of it was in ruins, but visitors who had paid their entrance fee could explore the various rooms and towers and courtyard.

There were worn, stone steps leading down to the dungeons where prisoners had once been chained to the wall and fed on bread and water. A heavy chain was still fixed to the wall, rusty with age. There was a small window, high in the dungeon wall, with iron bars across it. The sun was shining when Simon's father took him to visit the castle, but it did not shine into the dungeon. Here the air felt cold and damp and rather creepy, and there were green stains on the walls, and drops of water trickling down.

Simon was glad when they climbed the staircase back into the sunshine. There were sea gulls wheeling around and pink flowers growing on the short green turf.

There was a well in the courtyard, fifty feet deep, with a grating over it so that no one could fall in. People dropped pebbles through the grating and Simon dropped a small white stone he had in his pocket. It was many seconds before he heard the splash as it reached the surface of the water.

A keeper in uniform looked after the castle, and took the visitors' money and gave them tickets. He also sold postcards. Simon bought a card of the dungeon and sent it to his old friend in Flat 5.

School was as different as his new house. There were not as many children, and the teachers did not seem to shout or give as many punishments. Even mathematics, which Simon dreaded, was not so terrible after all, and a wrong answer did not seem to matter. Best of all, the other boys and girls were friendly.

He admired a bigger boy with a mop of curly black hair, called Julian, who was the leader of a group. He was very proud when Julian came up to him one day and said, "Would you like to join my gang?"

"Yes, I would," said Simon.

"You only have to swear never to tell tales, and to help any of the gang who are in trouble, and to do what I say."

"I swear," said Simon seriously.

"That's good. We usually meet at break and on Saturdays under the chestnut tree on the green."

Simon had wonderful times with Julian and his

gang. They often went on the beach and collected things washed up by the tide, especially if it had been a high one. They found driftwood and sponges and plastic bottles. Sometimes they threw a bottle back into the sea and skipped stones at it. They spent many hours throwing stones at rocks and breakwaters and posts.

Simon learned many things from Julian and his gang. He was fascinated by the stories they told him of the ghost who haunted the castle.

"It's a boy about like us," said Julian. "He was chained up in the dungeon and the old jailer was fetching him a jug of water when he fell into the well and was drowned. The lord of the castle was away fighting and no one knew the boy was there, so he slowly starved to death."

"What does the ghost do?" asked Simon. "Does he rattle his chain?"

"No, he whistles. I suppose he whistled when he was starving to try to keep his courage up. He'd need to do something, all alone in that damp, dark place, not knowing the time or the day of the week, or what had happened to his jailer, or anything."

"Who has seen him?"

"My grandmother heard him when she was a girl," said a boy named Frank. "She was coming home at midnight, after a dance, and as she passed the castle she heard this strange whistling. She told me she ran home like the wind and when she got to bed she lay and shivered all night long."

"My mother knows someone who heard the ghost,"

said another boy. "He was working in shifts and cycling home as the church clock struck twelve, and he heard someone whistling in the castle. It sounded all muffled as if it came from deep down."

Simon asked a great many questions, but he did not learn much more. The ghost was a young boy, and he could sometimes be heard whistling at midnight. No one had actually seen him.

"Mother," said Simon that evening, as he was having his supper, "why do ghosts appear at midnight?"

"I don't believe ghosts appear at all, at midnight or at any other time," she answered, "but midnight is sometimes called 'the witching hour,' because spirits of dead people are seen by the living at that time. But it's all rubbish."

"Mother, did you know there was a ghost in the castle?"

"No, I hadn't heard that there was, but I'm not surprised. I would be more surprised if there wasn't one. All old castles and many old houses are said to be haunted. People like to frighten themselves and each other by telling ghost stories, and there are lots of books about ghosts and ghouls and goblins."

Simon often thought of the whistling ghost when he was in bed, but he always fell asleep before he had thought for long. He imagined how *he* would have felt, chained up in that horrible dungeon, waiting for the footsteps of his jailer bringing him his daily bread and water. And then waiting for the footsteps that never came, and hearing only the cries of the sea gulls outside, and the waves breaking on the rocks below.

I wonder what tune he whistled, he thought. I suppose they had quite different songs and music hundreds and hundreds of years ago. I would have whistled *Pop Goes the Weasel*, but I don't whistle very well. He had plenty of time to practice, alone in the dungeon. I wonder what they shut him up for. A little boy couldn't have done anything so very wicked.

He asked the gang, the next day, why the young boy had been shut up. They were rather vague, but several boys said that the boy's father had been fighting against the lord of the castle and the lord was winning, so the father had to go into hiding. The boy knew where the hiding place was, but he wouldn't tell. So he was put into the dungeon to make him tell.

Some weeks later, Julian called a special meeting of what he called his committee, which consisted of those in the gang he depended upon most. Although Simon was the newest member, he had already been chosen to be on the committee. They met after school by table rock, which was a big, square rock hidden at high tide, but exposed at low tide with its fringe of seaweed and its crust of limpets.

There were five members of the gang, including Julian, and they were all there.

"This is something just for us," said Julian. "If we let in the whole gang, the grown-ups will get to know and the whole plan will be spoiled. Repeat your promise."

They repeated, "Word shall not pass my lips, nor fire nor water nor the powers of darkness shall make me tell. Cross my heart."

"It's full moon next Friday; it says so on our calendar. I vote we visit the cattle at midnight and try to hear the ghost whistling. We might even *see* him whistling because we wouldn't be frightened of a ghost. We wouldn't run away."

"I might be frightened of a ghost," said a quiet boy named Howard.

There were sympathetic murmurs at this.

"Well, I might be frightened myself, if I were alone," said Julian. "But we won't be alone. There'll be five of us. We won't be frightened when we're all together. Now who wants to come?"

"I do," cried all the committee.

"We'll meet outside the castle at ten to twelve by the church clock. We'll each bring a flashlight and wear gym shoes so as not to make a noise. And we'd better wear old clothes. We won't be able to see very well, and we might rub against that green slime on the stones, or something. Then our mothers might get suspicious. Now can you all get out safely?"

There were many problems here. Simon always fell asleep within a few minutes of settling down. One boy had a dog that barked at every strange sound. Another slept with a younger brother. Another had a front door that was bolted as well as locked, and the bolts were stiff.

But Julian was a born leader. He listened to everyone's problems and thought of ways of solving them. He sounded so confident that they felt confident, too. They decided to stay awake that night because once they were asleep they couldn't be sure of waking at the right time, not even if they banged their heads eleven times on the bedroom wall which was supposed to make you wake at eleven o'clock. No one dared use an alarm clock. It might wake the whole family.

"But how do we get into the castle?" asked Simon. "It's locked up at sunset."

Everyone laughed. "You don't mean to say you *paid* to go in?" they said in amazement. "There's a way in around the back. You scramble under the fence. It's dead easy. We've done it dozens of times."

Friday came and there was no sign of rain. They had decided it would be too risky to go if it were wet. Parents were bound to spot wet clothes and fuss and ask questions. The rest of the gang knew nothing because Julian had ordered no whispering in corners and no mysterious looks. When they went home after school, Julian merely said to the four gang members, "O.K.?" and they answered, "O.K., chief."

They planned to ask their parents if they could see a television program at 9 o'clock called, "Roads and Bridges." This went on till 10 o'clock and so quite a slice of evening would pass.

"I didn't know you were interested in roads and bridges," said Simon's father.

"I'm not, really, but it will be a help with my geography."

"Oh, well, if it's a help with your schoolwork, you can see it."

"And it's Friday night, so if I go to bed a bit late, I can sleep in tomorrow as it's Saturday."

Similar conversations were taking place in four

other homes, but they did not all end as successfully. Two fathers refused to switch from a comedy series and declared that roads and bridges could be studied as well from library books.

Simon **felt** wide awake as he lay in bed after the program and listened to the church clock, which chimed the quarters and half-hours as well as the hours. Though his mind was wide awake, part of him was very sleepy. Once or twice he even dropped off and woke with a terrible start. Supposing it were after twelve and he was too late? He switched on his flashlight and looked at his bedroom clock. What, only half-past ten! Surely he had been awake for hours and hours. Supposing the clock had stopped? No, it was ticking busily away.

He began, yet again, to say his tables and all the hymns and poems he could remember. But always, in the darkness, he glimpsed a pale, cloudy figure with white cheeks and great, staring eyes.

At last it was half-past eleven and Simon thankfully got out of bed and put on his old jeans and a thick sweater and his gym shoes. He checked his flashlight which was fitted with a new battery. It was a very special flashlight, for by moving a catch at the side it could shine with a red light or a green.

The stairs hardly creaked as he tiptoed down them, and the lock, carefully oiled earlier in the week, turned silently. He left the latch up so that he could easily open the door on his return. Taking the key with him was too much of a risk. He might lose it.

When he reached the castle gates, Julian was already there, and two other boys appeared in a few minutes. But there was no sign of Frank.

"Gone to sleep, I expect," said Julian. "I said we wouldn't wait after ten to twelve and we won't. Follow me."

The three boys kept close to Julian as he led them around to the back of the castle, which was the seaward side. He suddenly crouched down and wriggled under the fence. The others followed. The moonlight was so bright that they did not need their flashlights. Inside the castle it was darker, and the steps down into the dungeon were difficult to see.

"Flashlights, boys," ordered Julian, shining his own on the worn, twisting stairs. Soon they were all inside the dungeon.

"Flashlights off. Absolutely still. Just wait."

Julian spoke in a whisper, but they all heard and obeyed. Then the church clock struck twelve. They counted the strokes. At first they could only hear their own hearts beating and the sound of the waves breaking. Then, from nearby, came a clear, unmistakable whistle.

The committee did not need to discuss what to do next. They found themselves flying up the stone stairs like a herd of startled deer, scraping their shins painfully on jutting pieces of rock and pushing into each other. The chief fled with his men, knees trembling and breath coming in short gasps.

When they were well clear of the castle, Julian said

uncertainly, "Anyone like to go back and investigate?"

There were murmurs of, "No, not on your life!" and the white-faced committee went off to their various homes. As Simon opened the gate of *Wave Crest,* he suddenly realized that he had dropped his flashlight in the mad scramble. Unfortunately there was no one else in sight or he would have tried to persuade them to come back with him.

He wondered whether to leave the flashlight where it was and fetch it another day. Then he felt sure that some visitor would find it before he could get there, as

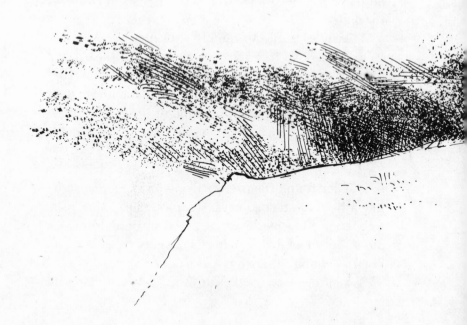

cars were always rolling up full of sightseers. It was such a very special flashlight, a present on his tenth birthday, and it was the envy of the whole gang. He must get it back. But how?

By now he was breathing normally and his knees had stopped shaking. He remembered his mother's voice saying confidently, "Ghosts are all rubbish."

Of course the whistling wasn't rubbish, that was real, and they had all heard it. But after all, they hadn't *seen* anything, not a glimpse of the whistling boy. Perhaps he only whistled at midnight and it was now after quarter-past twelve. The more Simon thought about his fantastic flashlight the more he wanted it back. And he wanted it back now.

Slowly and silently he made his way to the castle and wriggled under the fence. Slowly he approached the entrance to the dungeon, listening all the time. If he heard the merest echo of a whistle, he would run away. But there was nothing to hear, only the waves.

Very slowly, step by step, he walked down the dark, deep stairs, wishing he had his flashlight to help him. At the bottom he paused and listened again. Still no sound. Just then his foot struck against something that rolled along the stone floor with a clatter. It was his flashlight. He must have dropped it the minute he had heard the ghostly whistle.

Simon stooped down to pick it up, and as he stooped he heard, just by his ear, in fact in his ear, a whistle. Holding his flashlight tightly this time, he ran up the stairs and made for the fence, slipped under it, and headed for home. He scarcely thought of what he had just heard—he simply ran.

Soon there were four boys huddled in their beds with a great deal to think of and Simon had the most of all, but before the clock struck one all were fast asleep.

The next morning Simon got up earlier than usual, though his parents expressed surprise at this.

"Sitting up late seems to agree with you," said his father. "As you are so energetic, perhaps you'll help me with some gardening."

"I will this afternoon, Dad, but I must see Julian this morning. I promised."

Simon did not wait for the usual Saturday meeting of the gang under the chestnut tree; he went around to Julian's house.

"I must see you, Julian. Can you come out?"

"Yes, of course. I wanted to see you too."

"Say, chief," began Simon, when they were safely out of the house, "I've got something important to tell you." And he related his adventure when he went back for his flashlight. Julian listened intently.

"You say when you stooped down someone whistled *in* your ear?"

"Yes. Right in my ear. I felt his breath."

"Then we must both go back into the dungeon and investigate, in the daylight, of course."

"Of course," agreed Simon. "Let's go now."

"We won't tell the other boys in the committee."

"All right. If we go now, the guard will be making a cup of tea in his hut. He always makes one when he first goes on duty. Then he can't spy on us."

They slipped into the castle. Seen together, in daylight, the dungeon was not as alarming, though even daylight could not get rid of the chill in the air or the green stains on the wall.

"I was standing about here," said Simon, "and I stooped down like this."

"Then your ear was about here," said Julian. "Look, there's a kind of chink between the stones, like a deep crack. It's too narrow for my hand."

"Let me have a go. My hand is smaller." Simon was a thin boy with skinny hands and arms. He rolled up his sleeve and squeezed his hand into the crevice.

"I can feel something—honest I can. Just a second, and I'll get it out."

After some fumbling he brought out his hand, unaware that his knuckles were bleeding where he had grazed them, and held out a small object.

"Whatever is it?" asked Julian.

"It's a bone."

"It's a bone with a hole through it."

"Someone made the hole, I'm sure."

"*He* made it. He must have made it and hidden it in the secret crack."

"He wouldn't want the jailer to see it or he might have taken it away."

"And it was all he had to play with."

"But—but the whistling? I know I heard it. I swear I heard it," said Simon.

Julian put the bone to his lips and blew. A thin sound emerged, a ghostly whistle.

"But Julian, how could *he* blow it last night? I mean—well—how could he?"

They stood a few minutes, thinking hard. Then a light dawned on Julian's face.

"It was the wind, the wind blowing off the sea. It blew through the crack and through the bone. You said you could feel a breath in your ear."

"So I could."

"And it made a whistling noise."

They stood side by side, Simon fingering the whistle. Each was thinking of a little boy like themselves, chained in a dungeon, with just one thing to play with, a precious bone whistle which had to be kept hidden from the watchful jailer.

"What will you do with it?" asked Julian.

"Put it back where I found it."

Simon slipped the bone back into its hiding place and began to suck his knuckles which were beginning to smart.

"Shall we tell the committee?"

"Not yet," said Simon. "If he could keep the whistle a secret, then so can we. Let's hurry or the guard will have finished his tea."

The Cat Who Liked Children

"It's happened again," said Prue to Adam.

"The same place?" said Adam.

"Yes, exactly. Come quickly before it gets cold."

They ran up the stairs, which were still without carpets as the family had just moved in, and Adam followed Prue into her bedroom, which was at the end of a passage.

Here, things were in better order. There was no rug on the floor, but otherwise it was like an ordinary bedroom. Both children ran to the bedside. On the hump the pillow made there was a hollow in the pink bedspread. Adam put his hand in the hollow.

"Quite warm," he said.

"I told you so, I told you so," said Prue. "That's exactly how it has been twice before. The dent in the pillow and the warmth."

She put her hand where his had been.

"It can't be the sun, as there isn't any today," said Adam.

"Anyhow," went on Prue, "the sun couldn't pick out

just one small spot to shine on, and leave the rest of the bed cold."

"And it's so round."

"It's what I've always told you it was," said Prue. "It's the kind of warmth a cat leaves behind when it has been curled up asleep."

"When did you make your bed, Prue?"

"Directly after breakfast, when I cleaned my teeth. That was over an hour ago."

"Could a cat have got in somehow?"

"The window is only open a crack at the top because it was so cold last night. And I found the door shut."

They opened the window at the bottom and looked out. The lawn below was silvered with frost, and the ivy leaves on the wall were furred around the edge.

"Even if it climbed up the wall, it couldn't have got in."

"Shall we tell Mother?"

"Not yet. Perhaps we shall find out more. And by now the hollow will be getting cool. We've left it too late."

For the next few days there was a great deal for everybody to do, moving into a strange house. The children had books and toys to arrange, and they were always being sent to the village shop on their bicycles for twelve cup hooks or a ball of strong string. They didn't mind these errands because everything was different and enjoyable. The ride downhill made up for having to push their bicycles some of the way home, and Mrs. Becky at the shop was so kind and friendly. She sold almost everything they could think of, even sealing wax and chocolate fudge.

One day, when the sitting room was straight, the children went into it to drink their cocoa by the fire. At once they noticed that a cushion on the sofa had a hollow in it, and they soon found that the hollow was warm.

"So it comes in here, too," said Adam.

"The warmest place," said Prue, "except for the kitchen. I wonder if it has left a hair behind."

Their cocoa cooled while they searched. Then Adam found one fine black hair.

"It's a black cat. That's lucky," said Prue.

"No, it only means that it has some black on it," said Adam, who liked to get things right. "It could easily be black and white."

When they took their empty mugs into the kitchen, they found their mother stooping down, looking at a table leg.

"I said the moving men were simply wonderful, handling everything so carefully, but look at these scratches," she said.

They looked, and saw that the table leg was covered with scratches.

"It's as though a cat had been sharpening her claws," said their mother. "I've never noticed them before. I suppose you children don't know anything about it?"

"Oh, no," said Adam and Prue truthfully. "We didn't do it."

"The other three legs haven't any scratches," said Adam.

"That makes it seem more like a cat," said their mother. "Cats usually choose one favorite place for scratching."

"What do we do next?" said Prue, when she was alone with Adam. "Shall we set a trap?"

"A trap to catch a ghost!"

"Oh, I don't mean a trap to catch it. I mean—well, I mean a kind of trick to make it show itself. We could put down some food and watch to see if it eats it."

"Ghosts don't eat food," said Adam.

"This cat might," said Prue. "And it may not be a ghost. It may be a very, very clever—"

"Frightened—"

"Hungry—"

"Ordinary—"

"Cat."

They fetched two saucers from Prue's doll's tea set. It was easy enough to get milk, but fish was different. They had to wait till Wednesday when the fish van called, and they had fish for lunch. Adam hid some of his helping in his handkerchief and afterwards they prepared the milk and the fish.

"Where can we leave it?" said Prue. "Mother is sure to see it."

"We can leave it behind the sofa. The cat will smell it. And Mother is going to tidy the box-room this afternoon. She said so."

The saucers were left behind the sofa, and Prue

watched from the window seat. She had a book on her lap, but she kept one eye on the food. Adam said he'd take her place after an hour. Then their mother called, "Children, come quickly. I want to ask you something."

They both ran upstairs and found her holding up a pair of roller skates.

"Tell me, aren't these too small? May I send them to a jumble sale?"

"Yes, do," said the children quickly, irritated at being interrupted, and vanished downstairs, hearing their mother calling out, "You might at least have tried them on."

They crept into the sitting-room and saw that both saucers were empty. There were a few drops of milk scattered around one saucer."

"It splashes," said Adam.

"Or shakes its whiskers," said Prue. She picked up the empty saucers, but stood with them in her hands.

"Adam, listen. I can hear something."

They both stood, listening.

"It's the clock," said Adam.

"It's the clock, and—" said Prue. "Listen again."

They both heard a soft, low, murmuring sound.

"It's purring," said Adam.

"I know," said Prue. "She's happy. Puss! Puss! Puss! Where are you? Where are you, pussy?"

The purring went on, but there was nothing to see in the room except themselves.

"She purrs. She eats and drinks. She sleeps in comfortable places. Do you think she'll ever let us see her?"

"I don't know," said Adam. "We're bound to catch sight of her some time or other if she's real. And if she's not—"

"If she's not?" asked Prue.

"Well, it doesn't make sense. She must be real."

They tried to tempt the cat with food again. The food disappeared while Prue and Adam were changing places. The next time their mother found it.

"I don't know what on earth you're doing, but I can't have food in here, especially food on the carpet. Take it away at once. Why, it smells like fish."

"We're pretending we have a cat," said Prue boldly.

"Then you must feed it on pretend food," said their mother firmly. "Go and throw this out to the birds."

One day a friend called with a cocky little black and white terrier.

"Lie down," said his mistress. "Lie down, Punch."

But Punch would not lie down. He prowled about the room, his back bristling, making short, sharp rushes, and barking.

"Don't be so crazy," said his mistress. "You'd think there was a cat in the room. He always bristles like that when he smells a cat. I'll have to shut him up in the car."

Punch was carried off protesting, and when he was in the car, he still barked. The children looked at each other. So Punch knew, too. This made the cat even more real, and even more mysterious.

Time went by, and as the days grew **warmer the**

children played more and more in the garden. But seldom a day passed without one of them finding a warm hollow where the cat had slept, or hearing her purr with happiness. Twice they found a fine black hair which Prue felt proved she was a black cat, but Adam still maintained that it might be black and white. Somehow, the longer they lived in the house, the more ordinary the cat seemed. Once Prue was sure something silent and furry brushed past her legs when she opened a door.

"I wonder why she never says meow," said Adam. "Most cats meow when they want things."

"This cat doesn't want anything," said Prue. "She's a happy, purring cat. She knows we love her."

One day, their mother gathered a big bunch of daffodils from the garden. "Will one of you take these to Miss Swan?" she said. "She'll be missing all her spring flowers."

Miss Swan was the old lady from whom they had bought the house. It was far too large for her and she had moved to a cottage in the village where she had only window boxes to take care of.

"Yes, I will!" said Adam and Prue together.

Their mother looked surprised. The children were not usually very anxious to visit old ladies, particularly ones they hardly knew.

"Then you'd better both go," she said. "Don't forget to ask Miss Swan to come and see the garden, and of course us, whenever she'd like."

Adam put the flowers in his bicycle basket and they rode off.

"If she invites us in, we'll go," said Prue, "and ask her about cats."

"We mustn't tell her about our cat," said Adam. "She might laugh."

"But our cat may have been her cat once," said Prue. "We'll try to find out. Don't leave all the talking to me. You must back me up."

Miss Swan did ask them in, and they found themselves sitting side by side on the sofa. A large marmalade cat was sleeping in front of the fire.

"Did your cat once live in our house?" asked Adam.

"Yes, my dear, he lived there nearly ten years. When we moved here, I buttered his paws so that he'd settle and not keep going back. And he has settled—he's quite at home as you can see."

"Have you always had a cat?" asked Prue.

"Yes, almost always."

"Will you tell us about them?"

Miss Swan poked the fire, and then began.

"There was a striped tabby, Polly, who used to catch the goldfish out of the pond. We had to give them away, those that were left. Then there was Polly's son, Tiger, a great climber and sad to say a great hunter, too. And then there was her grandson, another tabby, who scratched the furniture dreadfully."

"Were all your cats tabbies?" asked Adam.

"Most of them. We had a very valuable silver-gray

one who was always catching cold. In the end she died of bronchitis."

"But Miss Swan, have you never had a black cat?" said Prue.

"Or a black and white one?" added Adam.

A faraway look came into Miss Swan's blue eyes.

"Long, long ago, when I was just a child, I had a black cat called Gipsy. She must have been born in the woods as she was quite wild. It took me weeks and weeks to tame her, little by little, and at last she would let me touch her. She even came into the house for food, in the end, but she never could bear grown-ups. She vanished out of the door or a window whenever one of my parents came near. Anybody's footsteps, except mine, terrified her, though she became fond of my brothers and sisters. She used to sharpen her claws on one particular leg of the kitchen table and the cook got very annoyed. But no one ever saw her doing it. She was so clever. The cook said she'd give her what for if she caught her at her tricks, but she never did catch her."

"What happened to Gipsy?"

"Something very sad. She disappeared. She may have gone back to the woods, or perhaps she was caught in a trap. For a long time afterwards I used to wake in the night and hear her purring. Sometimes I felt her fur in the darkness. But when I woke up, there was nothing except a warm place on the bed. My father gave me a dog to comfort me. He was a jolly little

Scottie, and I never dreamed of Gipsy again. He must have frightened her away."

"Mother says please come and see the garden whenever you like," said Adam.

"Good-bye," said Prue. "I did like hearing about your cat who liked children."

They cycled home, wondering.

"What will happen when we grow up and aren't children anymore?" said Prue.

"Oh, let's not worry. I'm going on being a child for ages and ages. Race you from the next tree to the front gate."

The Silent Visitor

David and his sister Judith often went with their parents to visit their granny who lived a hundred miles away, in a house full of treasures. At least the children thought they were treasures. She had a china lady who nodded her head, an old dolls' house with quaintly dressed dolls sitting on little frilly chairs, and a cuckoo clock in the hall.

But this time when they got into the car to visit her, the trunk piled with their luggage, everything felt different from usual. Granny had been ill and was still not well enough to have a house full of visitors. They would see her every day, of course, but they were going to stay at a hotel in the village.

David and Judith had never before stayed at a hotel. They had had tea in one, when they were away on vacation, but they had never slept there. This made them excited and curious.

"There will be lots and lots of huge armchairs and sofas and carpets," said Judith.

"And the bedrooms will be very grand," said David.

"Mother says there'll be a washbasin in mine and a fire to put on if I'm cold and it won't go on till we've put money in a machine."

"I wish I were sleeping with you," said Judith, "like I do at Granny's. Then we could play in the morning if we wake early. I love sleeping in the attic at Granny's, with the treetops just outside the window and the wallpaper with roses on it."

"I'm glad I'm sleeping alone," said David. "I'm getting too old to share my bedroom with a girl."

"Then you're too old to share my crayons or my candy," said Judith sharply, grabbing a packet of jelly beans.

"I'm not. That's different." David tried to grab back and soon they were fighting.

"Stop scuffling," said Daddy crossly. "I won't drive with all that commotion going on. Stop it at once, or I shall take the wretched candy away."

The children stopped immediately. Daddy always meant what he said. But Judith stuck her tongue out at her brother, and he made a monkey face back at her.

"I'll tell you all I know about the hotel," said Mother peacefully, "though it isn't very much. It's a very, very old building; I believe four hundred years old. It has low, dark rooms with beams across the ceiling and small windows, and rather uneven floors. Daddy and I once went there for a drink. It has lights like lanterns and a sign outside of a coach and horses. That's its name."

"It isn't at all grand," added Daddy. "Rather dark and poky. But I dare say we shall be comfortable enough. You children and I will be out all day and your mother will be spending a good deal of her time with Granny."

The rest of the journey went well. They picnicked by a bridge, and the children floated sticks in the water. Judith decided to let David share her crayons, and they did some coloring.

The children thought the *Coach and Horses* looked lovely. A lady showed them to their rooms; a big room for their parents, a little room opening out of it for Judith, and a room at the end of the corridor for David. They all went to see Granny, then they had dinner, and then it was their bedtime. Judith was tucked in first as she was the younger, and then David.

"You'll be all right?" asked Mother as she kissed him.

"Yes," said David doubtfully.

"You know how to switch on your bedside light, and you've got your books and your little cars for the morning?"

"Yes."

"And you know where our room is, Number 9."

"Yes, but the passage will be dark."

"No, it won't, darling. Lights are left on all night in hotels."

"Then I'm all right," beamed David, settling down into a very large, soft pillow.

Though David was warm and comfortable, he for some reason or other. *Creak!* There it was again. in the main street outside and the furniture creaked couldn't get off to sleep. There was the noise of cars

David began to think he could hear someone breathing. He quickly switched on the light. No, all was well. He switched it off again.

At 9 o'clock, as he counted the strokes of the church clock, Mother came in.

"Not asleep, David?"

"No. And I never will be."

"Are you warm?"

"Yes. But something keeps creaking."

"It's probably the floor, or that old cupboard. Old wood gets very dry and creaks."

She gave him a drink of water and plumped up his pillow.

"I'll look in again when we come up to bed."

David still could not get to sleep, though he did not mind the creaks so much. He wondered whether to turn his light on and play with his cars. But he felt too comfortable to sit up.

When his parents came to bed they both looked in.

"Not asleep yet?"

"No, but I will be soon. I'm very sleepy."

"You can always come to our room," said Daddy, "and we'll change beds. You can have mine and I'll have yours. You might sleep better with company. You're used to having Judith."

David certainly felt very drowsy, though he could not quite drop off. Some time later Mother crept in. She didn't say a word, but laid a cool hand on his forehead and settled the bedclothes around his shoulders. She crept away, and he fell asleep instantly.

Both children slept late the next day, and David did not wake till his mother came to tell him it was time to get up.

Breakfast was a delicious meal. They could choose porridge or one of three cereals, and they began with ice-cold fruit juice. Then there was a choice of bacon or different kinds of egg. David chose scrambled because it was his favorite. Judith chose bacon.

"Did you get to sleep quickly after we went to bed?" Mother asked David.

"Not very. But when you crept back quietly and settled the bedclothes, I just dropped off."

"But I never came back after Daddy and I said good night."

"You did. You didn't say anything, but you put your hand on my forehead and tucked me in."

"You must have dreamed it," said Daddy.

"I didn't. I know I didn't. I couldn't see Mother because she didn't put the light on. It wasn't a dream, so there! I know when I'm asleep or awake." David sounded cross.

"Well, if it was a dream, it was a lovely one," said Mother. "Just the kind of dream I'd like to have myself. Now eat up your scramble. Daddy thought he'd take you both on the river in a boat."

"Oh, good. Can we learn to row?"

"I doubt whether you're big enough, but you and Judith can try sharing an oar," said Daddy.

The next few days went by very quickly. The children were out all day with their father. Sometimes Mother came, too, and sometimes she went to see Granny. The children visited Granny every day, but they did not stay long. She was so thin that once her wedding ring rolled off and Judith had to poke it from under the sofa. But she was as nice as always, wanting to know all about their pet hamster, and David's school, and Judith's play-group.

One night Judith was sick, and the next day she

was hot and uncomfortable. She occasionally had these sick turns which lasted for twenty-four hours or so. She stayed in bed, and Mother stayed in the hotel to look after her. Daddy took David to a Railway Museum in the next town where he could not only look at the old engines but actually climb into the cab and pretend to drive. They were quite different from the diesels that were used nowadays.

When they got back, Mother went off to see Granny and Daddy and David played card games.

"Judith has gone to sleep," said Mother as she left. "Her bed's in an awful muddle, half the clothes are on the floor, and she's lying across it, but I didn't like to disturb her. She'll probably be all right when she wakes up."

When Mother came back from seeing Granny, she went straight up to Judith. She came down and said to Daddy in a puzzled voice, "How did you manage to make her bed so beautifully without waking her?"

"I didn't" said Daddy. "I went up twice, but each time she was lying in a frightful muddle, just as you said, with half the clothes on the floor."

"Then the maid must have done it. Kind of her, but quite unnecessary. I shall speak to her."

Mother went upstairs again and found the maid, Marie, turning down the beds.

"Oh, Marie, thank you for straightening Judith's bed, but I really didn't want her disturbed. She had a bad night, and I wanted her to sleep on."

"But madam, I never even went into Judith's room.

I wouldn't do that. And I knew that Mr. Mills and your son were in the hotel. Why look, I haven't even turned your bed down yet."

"You're quite sure, Marie, because my husband hasn't touched Judith's bed?"

"Neither have I. I know my duties." And Marie flounced off.

Mrs. Mills met the hotel manager, Mr. Grey, in the hall.

"Mr. Grey, I'm sorry to bother you, but there's something that's puzzling me. You know my little girl is in bed because she's been poorly?"

"Why, yes. I do hope she's better."

"Yes, thank you. It was only a mild tummy upset. But someone has gone into her room and straightened up her bed while she was asleep. You know they would have to go through our room first."

"Have you asked Marie?"

"Yes, and she says she hasn't been into the room."

"Then she hasn't. Marie is completely dependable and has been with us for twenty years."

"Could any other member of the staff have been upstairs?"

"That's not possible. Only Marie has duties on that floor at this time. But I'll ask, of course."

He looked a little uncomfortable as he went into his office, as if something were on his mind.

When Judith woke up, she was much better and even had a little supper of orange juice and brown bread and butter. When asked if anyone strange had been into her room and tidied her bed, she only said,

"I believe someone did come in and fiddle around. But I was really asleep. I didn't open my eyes. She didn't say anything, but I think she laid her hand on my head. I remember because her hand was so cool."

"Strange," said Mr. Mills with a laugh, when he was alone with his wife. "Now both children have had mysterious visitors with cool hands. I shall expect someone to come and visit *me* tonight and lay a cool hand on my head."

"I wish them joy," said Mrs. Mills. "You wouldn't wake for a cool hand, nor yet for an icy one. Why, even the alarm clock doesn't wake you!"

The next day Judith got up as usual, but her mother decided that she had better have a quiet day and spend it with Granny. Judith liked this idea as she hadn't had time, yet, to play with the dolls' house. She particularly liked a little fur cat that lay curled up on a rug in the kitchen, and she wanted to move him onto one of the beds for a treat.

"We'll do just what you like." said Daddy to David. "It's raining cats and dogs, so we'd better not get too wet or Mother won't be pleased."

"Do you think we could possibly—but you'd be bored," added David regretfully.

"Out with it. It takes a lot to bore me."

"Do you think we could go to the Railway Museum again?"

"Of course we can. A very good idea. I'll bring *The Times* so I can do the crossword if I get tired of looking around."

That evening Judith did not stay up for dinner. She

went to bed at six and Marie brought her a tray of soup and egg sandwiches. She dropped off to sleep soon afterwards, managing, as usual, to untuck her bed-clothes and screw her pillow into a ball. Mother always had to straighten the bed up later.

There was half-an-hour before dinner, and Mrs. Mills lay on her bed with her library book. Then she got up to change her dress and wash her hands. She peeped in at Judith. A moment later she was running down-stairs to find her husband. David was playing with his cars on the lounge windowsill.

"Don, something very queer has happened. Some-thing rather frightening."

"Tell me, darling."

"I was actually in our room, lying on my bed with a book, and someone passed through—but how could they?—and tidied Judith's bed again. I'd looked just before I had my rest and she was asleep in her usual muddle, all untucked and higgledy-piggledy. Then when I looked after I'd changed for dinner, she was neat as a pin."

"You're sure no one came through while you were having a little doze?"

"I'm absolutely sure. I was reading a very exciting thriller, and I couldn't possibly have dozed."

"Judith's room has two doors, the one into our room and a second one into the passage."

"But the landing door is bolted on the inside. I looked. It's a very strong bolt, too."

"Don't worry, dear. We'll talk about it when David

is in bed. Remember, no harm has been done. The child hasn't been hurt or frightened. I suppose she couldn't have tidied her bed herself?"

"Don't be funny. A child just six couldn't tuck in blankets and smooth sheets as neatly as that. She just wouldn't know how."

When David was in bed, Mr. and Mrs. Mills had a long talk. Then they went off together to the manager's office. He was alone.

"Mr. Grey, can you spare a few minutes?"

"Of course, Mr. Mills. I hope the hotel is proving comfortable?"

"Oh yes. Perfectly. It isn't anything like that that's worrying us."

They told Mr. Grey about the mysterious person who had gone into Judith's room, invisibly, while Mrs. Mills was lying on her own bed.

Mr. Grey looked more and more uncomfortable while they were telling their story. He tapped his fingers on the desk and shifted uneasily in his chair.

"Mr. Grey," said Mrs. Mills, leaning forward, "I'm sure you know something about this that you're keeping from us. Please, please, tell us all you know. No harm has been done to our children. They haven't been distressed or upset. But surely we have a right to know. Please be open with us."

Mr. Grey fidgeted more than ever and shifted his gaze from one to the other.

"There is something perhaps I ought to tell you, but there's my hotel to think of, and my reputation. Business will melt away if there are any rumors. You appreciate that."

"Whatever you tell us we shall treat as confidential and never pass it on, unless it concerns the well-being of any of your guests."

"Then I'll tell you. I'll make a clean breast of it. You know this hotel is very old and was first built in the fifteenth century as a private house. A Lord and Lady Blackett lived here with their seven children. They say that Lord Blackett was away at the wars and Lady Emma was left behind with their children. There was a terrible epidemic—some say cholera—and all the children caught it. The poor lady never went to bed, but moved from room to room with a candle in her hand, trying to sooth and comfort the children. All the servants had left her on account of the cholera."

He paused.

"What happened?" asked Mrs. Mills.

"They all died, all seven of them. And then the poor lady took ill and died herself. Their tomb is in the church, in the north transept."

"How tragic. But you haven't finished the story?"

"Well, the ghost of Lady Emma is supposed to walk. She only settles the bedclothes more comfortably around people's shoulders and lays her hand on their foreheads. She does no harm. She is especially concerned with little children."

"Have many of your guests experienced this—this phenomenon?"

"Quite a few, over the years. But only those sleeping

in the wing where you and the children are. That is the oldest, original part of the house. All the other rooms are more recent."

"I don't think I shall sleep tonight," said Mrs. Mills as they lay in bed. "Perhaps the poor Lady Emma will take pity on me and come and settle me and lay her cool hand on me."

"It's a strange legend," said her husband, "strange and haunting. Tomorrow I would like to visit the tomb. I've been in the church several times, but I've never noticed it."

The next day, David and Judith visited Granny, and she was well enough to play dominoes with them. Judith had just learned how to play, and was very pleased with herself. The other two often had to wait while she counted the spots.

Mr. and Mrs. Mills went to the church to look at the Blackett tomb. They found it at once, in the north transept, as Mr. Grey had said. It was made of alabaster and was oblong, with statues of Lord Blackett and Lady Emma lying on top, as if on a bed. The Lord was wearing armor, and Lady Emma a long, flowing robe with a curving headdress from which hung a veil. Her shoes were very pointed.

Along one side of the tomb a row of children was carved, kneeling with their hands together. Three boys knelt on one side facing four girls, who knelt opposite.

"Poor woman," said Mrs. Mills. "What a lovely face and what a sad death. Seven little children!"

"And poor father," added Mr. Mills, "coming home

from the war to find an empty house, no wife, and no child."

They stood there for a few minutes looking down at the tomb, thinking their own thoughts. Then they slowly left the church and went into the sunshine, ready to join their children.

Mirror, Mirror on the Wall

In winter, a heavy blue curtain was drawn across the front door to keep out the drafts. A girl named Jane liked to hide behind it. There was nothing and no one to hide from. No one was playing hide-and-seek with her, or looking for her. But she hid there because she chose to.

As Jane crouched behind the soft velvet curtain, she could draw the edge a little to one side, and peep out. By doing this, she saw the gilt-framed mirror in the hall, which reflected a little of the hall itself, and half of the flight of stairs. The mirror looked so beautiful, like a pool of clear water, and the stairs looked beautiful, too, painted white, with dark blue carpet to walk on.

She could also see, if she leaned out, the edge of the curtain and her hand holding it. She looked very pale and small in the mirror, and her hair looked very fair. She looked much paler and smaller and fairer than she really was.

Without moving the curtain she could see her

mother going up or down stairs, and she could see her father when he came home from work. He always came in the back door as it was nearer to the garage. Her mother met him in the hall and kissed him. She always said, "Had a good day, dear?"

And he always replied, "Quite good, but busy."

When her cousin Maggie came to stay, they both hid behind the curtian, but Maggie soon got tired of being there.

"This curtain is smothering me," she cried. "Let's jump out at your mother when she comes into the hall and give her a fright. Or we'll wait and jump out at your father. That will be fun."

"I don't want to," said Jane. "If we do that, they'll know where we are, and I like my hiding places to be kept secret."

"Oh, please yourself," said Maggie crossly. "I'm going to ride on your rocking horse."

Jane watched her in the mirror, running upstairs in her scarlet tights. Maggie hadn't a rocking horse at home and she was never tired of riding on Jane's. He had black spots and a red bridle and saddle. He had gleaming black eyes, too, and a black mane.

Jane liked playing with Maggie, but she did not mind when she went home. Then she could go back to hiding in peace, looking into the mirror where everything was the same, yet different.

One evening, when Jane was behind the curtain, she felt a little bit sleepy. Perhaps it was rather stuffy behind its soft folds. As she looked out at the gilt-framed mirror, the glass clouded over in an odd way. When the glass cleared, she saw somebody, not her mother, going up the stairs. It was a strange woman in a white apron, with a white cap on her head. She was dragging a boy by the hand, a boy about Jane's age.

"Now come along," said the woman sharply. "It's past your bedtime. Don't make such a to-do, Master Abel. I'm ashamed of you."

"But I wanted to see Polly have her calf. Jones said it would be by morning. I wanted to see if it would be black and white like Polly, or all white like its father."

"Oh fie, Master Abel, the barn is no place for you. No wonder you're all plastered with mud. Now come along, or I shan't leave the candle alight when I say good night."

This mild threat had an instant effect on the boy. He stopped pulling and followed the woman quietly upstairs. He was wearing a striped jacket with a lace collar, and long, striped trousers. His shoes had silver buckles on them.

Poor Abel, thought Jane. He's afraid of the dark as I used to be. I remember always having my bedroom door ajar, and crying if anyone switched off the landing light by mistake. I wonder why I don't mind now?

Then she saw her father come in and greet her mother, and she slipped out of her hiding place and ran into the sitting room to kiss him.

"Have you ever heard of a boy called Abel?" she asked.

"Only in the Bible," said her father.

"I met one today," said Jane.

"Do you mean at school?"

"No. Not at school. In the looking glass."

"You mean you heard a story about Abel?"

"Not exactly, Daddy. Let's play one game of checkers before I go to bed. We'll just have time. You can be black and I'll be red."

A few nights later Jane saw Abel again, when she was in her hiding place. He was wearing the same striped suit and lace collar, and he was having another tussle with the woman in the white cap and apron.

"No, Master Abel, you can't take your hobbyhorse upstairs. It's not meant to go into your bedchamber. You've been riding it outside and it's muddy."

"But I love my hobbyhorse, Patty, and I want it to stand beside my bed. I won't get to sleep if I can't have it."

"Then you'll have to stay awake, won't you?" Patty snatched the horse from his grasp and dropped it down the stairs. Jane had a good view of it as it fell. It was a stick with a wooden horse's head on one end, and a bridle. It had bells somewhere because she heard them jingle.

Poor Abel, she thought again. How angry Patty seems. I wish he had someone like my mother to put him to bed. She wouldn't mind his having his horse in his bedroom. When I wanted my new bicycle to be near my bed, she asked Daddy to bring it up from the garage.

When her father came home, the mirror just reflected the stairs and hall as usual. She didn't ask any more questions about Abel. She kept him a secret, like the hiding place behind the curtain.

The next time Abel appeared, the scene was different. Jane had felt sleepy and the mirror had clouded over as before, when suddenly it cleared. She saw a man carrying something carefully in his arms. Patty followed behind, crying bitterly.

"He's dead," she sobbed. "He's dead."

"Now don't distress yourself," said the man. "His new pony threw him and kicked him between the eyes and he's in a swoon. Brown has ridden off for the physician. We must get him to bed and put a hot brick at his feet, and try to stop the bleeding with cold compresses."

"Poor little chap," said Patty. "I knew he was too young to ride that strong, nervous pony, but his father is so anxious for him to be manly."

"Manly indeed!" said the man. "He's a long way off being a man, poor child. Now make haste with the compresses while I lay him on the bed. He's losing a deal of blood."

Jane was horrified. Would Abel die? Would the physician come soon? Where was his mother? Everything seemed so slow. Why couldn't they have telephoned?

She stayed behind the curtain till she heard her father call out, "Where's Jane?"

Her mother answered, "Oh, playing around. She's always disappearing after tea. I think it's a kind of game. She's up to no harm."

Jane slipped out from behind the curtain and ran to her father.

"How's Abel today?" he asked, half-teasing.

"He's very, very ill. His pony kicked him."

"I believe you just make up stories about Abel."

"He *is* in a story, in a way. But it's not my story."

"Shall we have a game of checkers?"

"All right."

Jane fetched the board and the checkers, but she was thinking all the while of something else. She forgot when it was her turn and didn't see when there was a good move to be made. Her father won easily.

"You're a tired girl tonight," he said, as he kissed her. "A very tired girl."

Perhaps Jane was tired because she fell asleep soon after her mother turned out the light. At first she began to think about Abel, but her thoughts ran together in a jumble and then faded away. She slept deeply, without dreaming or moving. There was hardly a wrinkle in the bedclothes when, suddenly, she was awake. She had changed in a second from being deeply asleep to being absolutely wide awake.

Something had waked her, she was sure, but what? It was pitch dark, and it must have been very late because the landing light was turned off. That meant that her parents had gone to bed. She sat up and listened.

At first all was silent. Then she heard a low, moaning sound. She knew at once that it was a child crying quietly; a child trying not to cry. She got out of bed and put on her dressing gown and slippers, and started to walk down the passage. She passed the door of her parents' room. The bathroom. The spare room. Then she came to the playroom. The door had changed completely. Instead of being painted white, it was of some dark wood, with a heavy iron latch. She lifted the iron latch and went in.

The room had changed, too. Her rocking horse had gone, and her dolls' house, and all her other toys. The gas fire had gone, too. A coal fire was burning in the grate, and there was a rocking chair by the fire in which Patty was sitting. She was fast asleep, wrapped in a gray shawl, and snoring slightly. But Jane had no time to attend to Patty. Against the wall was a bed hung with curtains, and in this bed lay Abel, white as chalk, with a broad bandage across his forehead, covering his eyes. Jane tiptoed to his side and took one of his hot hands in hers.

"Is it very bad?" she whispered.

"Yes, it's pretty bad. I tried not to make a din and wake Patty."

"Shouldn't she be awake, and taking care of you?"

"She's tired out. She needs some sleep."

"Where is your mother?"

"My mother died when I was a baby."

"And your father?"

"My father is at the war. He is a soldier, a captain, and rides a great black horse. He's the best captain in the army, and the bravest."

"You're brave, too," said Jane. "I would be crying much worse if my pony had kicked me. I'd be screaming. I screamed and screamed when I shut my finger in the door and my nail came off."

"Well, you're a girl. You don't need to be brave.

You'll never have to go to the war and fight. But who are you? I've never seen you before."

"I'm Jane. I've seen you before. I saw you in the mirror."

"I don't understand. My head aches so much."

"I don't undestand either. Is your head very bad?"

"No, not so *very* bad. I was crying because Master Pepys, the physician, said I might lose my sight. I'd rather die than go blind."

"But Abel, if he said you might lose your sight, then it's just as likely that you might not. Let's believe that you won't be blind."

"All right, I'll try."

"Do your eyes hurt?"

"No. Caesar's hoof struck my brow, but Master Pepys said some nerve might be damaged. He didn't think I heard what he said. He was talking to Patty."

Patty stirred and the rocking chair creaked.

"I'll go now," whispered Jane.

"Come and see me tomorrow, please come."

"I'll come tomorrow if I can. And I'll think of you. I'll wish for your eyes to be all right."

She lifted the latch as quietly as she could, and went back to bed. The bed was still warm and she snuggled down under the blankets. She meant to think about Abel and the strange room and the coal fire, but she fell asleep instead.

The next thing she knew was that her mother was gently shaking her.

"I've let you sleep on, darling, and it's now ten o'clock. You must have been terribly tired. Do you feel quite well?"

Her mother put a cool hand on her forehead.

"I'm quite well, Mother. I feel absolutely well." And Jane jumped out of bed, dressed in a twinkling, and ate an extra large breakfast to prove it.

"There's nothing much wrong," said her mother, cutting Jane another slice of bread and honey. "You'd better go back to school this afternoon and I'll send a note to explain why you missed this morning."

That evening Jane did not hide behind the curtain and watch the gilt-framed mirror. She was sure there would be nothing special to see, only ordinary things. But she thought about Abel all the time, and hoped she would be able to see him that night.

Again, she slept deeply, and woke suddenly in the middle of the night. There was no sound of muffled crying this time. All was silent. She put on her dressing gown and slippers and went along the landing, past the familiar white doors, until she came to the heavy wooden one with the iron latch. Gently as she could, she lifted the latch and went in.

Patty was asleep in the rocking chair and the fire was glowing a dull red. A candle burned on the mantelpiece. She walked to the bedside and looked down at Abel. His face was still white with the bandage covering the upper part.

"Is it you, Jane?" he whispered, as she stood looking down.

"Yes, it is me. How are you?"

"I feel better, but I musn't move—not even to turn over in bed. I'm very weary. The hours seem like weeks."

"You poor boy. I wish I could come and visit you in the daytime, but—I don't know how. I only know the way in the night. Shall I tell you a story? Do you like exciting ones?"

"Thank you, Jane, but I'd rather talk."

"Yes, so would I."

Having decided to talk, at first neither of them had anything to say.

"Do you go to school?" said Jane.

"Not yet. But I may go soon."

"Then do you play all day, like I do on the holidays?"

"No, indeed. I have a tutor, Dr. Wynd. He teaches me Latin and Greek."

"How clever you must be! I won't do Latin till I'm

much older, perhaps twelve or thirteen, and I don't
suppose I shall ever learn Greek. Say some Latin to
me. I want to know what it sounds like."

"Facta non verba," said Abel.

"Whatever does that mean?"

"Deeds, not words."

"What else does Dr. Wynd teach you?"

"Why, nothing. But I shall do some mathematics
at school."

"Will you like school?"

"No, I shall hate it. Here I have my dogs and my
pony and the estate to roam about in. I shall lose my
freedom. And Dr. Wynd is gentle with me. The monitors
at school are very strict."

"But you'll enjoy the games," said Jane.

"What games?"

"Why, cricket and football and swimming."

"I've never heard of cricket and football, but I can
swim here in the river with the village boys. Or I could
if I was allowed. Tell me about your school."

Jane told him all she could about her school, and
the games they played at break, and how they played
ball games. Abel could hardly believe that the children
at Jane's school painted, and sang, and made things
out of clay.

"We have fun," went on Jane. "We dress up and
act plays, and it's lovely having stories. Doesn't Dr.
Wynd teach you to read and write?"

"Oh, I could do that before he came. The priest
taught me. I could read and write when I was four."

"Four!" exclaimed Jane. "I'm eight and I can only read and write easy words."

"Then you're a great dunce," said Abel.

"I'm not. I'm just like everyone else. How do your eyes feel?"

"I don't know. I try to open them under the bandage, but it's all dark."

"Of course it's dark under the bandage. It's like blind man's bluff."

"Oh, do you play that, too?" said Abel.

They were both pleased that they had something in common, if it was only blind man's bluff.

The logs in the fire settled with a slight noise. Patty moved her head.

"I must go now," whispered Jane. "I'll see you to-morrow."

The next evening Jane asked her father about the mirror in the hall.

"I don't know much about it," said her father, "except that it's old. It was Granny's once."

"Where did she get it from?"

"I think it was her mother's. I believe your great-grandfather bought it at a sale. He had a good eye for antiques. Do you like it?"

"I like it better than anything else in the whole house."

"I didn't know you were so vain," said her father.

"Oh, I don't look at myself in it, or hardly ever. I look at other people. It's so beautiful."

Jane got into the habit of visiting Abel every night.

She was always sleepy in the morning, but not as sleepy as she had been the first time. Once Patty was bending over the black kettle that stood on the fire, making a drink, and Jane withdrew. Once Abel was so fast asleep that she did not try to disturb him. But usually he heard her tiptoe in.

Then, one night, she found the door open and the chair by the fire empty.

"Patty has gone to sleep in her own chamber," said Abel. "I can ring if there is anything I want."

There was a little bell beside his bed, within easy reach.

"That's good. Then I can stay longer and we needn't whisper all the time."

They found many things to talk about, though Jane found that certain words puzzled Abel, and made him uneasy. If she mentioned the telephone or television, or said that her father had flown to Italy, he looked worried, almost frightened. She soon learned to avoid these words and they talked about books and pets and the garden. His garden was different from the one she played in, but both had an oak tree near the gate. They both knew Mr. Hutchinson's farm.

"It belongs to my father," said Abel.

"I think it belongs to Mr. Hutchinson now," said Jane.

"Why do you say 'now'?" asked Abel.

"I don't know. It just slipped out. Of course it's always 'now' when we're together. It must be."

One night Abel greeted Jane with the news that in

two days the bandage was to be removed from his eyes.

"Then you'll see."

"Then I *may* see," corrected Abel.

"You will see. I'll keep my fingers crossed for you."

The next night Jane said to Abel, "Hold out your hand. It's something nice, I promise."

She put something very tiny into it.

"What is it, Jane?"

"It's my lucky four-leaf clover. I've had it for ages. I found it at Granny's."

"Oh, thank you."

"Where will you put it to keep it safe?"

"I'll put it in my Bible, where the marker is."

The next night Jane's heart was beating fast as she opened Abel's door. The candle was burning on the mantelpiece, and she ran quickly to the bedside. A pair of large dark brown eyes looked up at her.

"Then it's all right? You can see me?"

"Yes, it's all right. I've got to be careful, but I won't be blind. Let me give you back your four-leaf clover."

"No, keep it. Perhaps it will help you to like school after all."

A few nights later Jane had difficulty in finding the heavy wooden door. She wandered up and down the passage almost in tears, when suddenly she found it, and lifted the latch and went in.

"I was ages finding you tonight, Abel. Ages and ages. What is happening?"

"I don't know, but don't give up coming to see me."

"Oh, I won't—unless I have to."

A week or so later Jane could not find the door any-where. She found her own playroom, with its white door and the rocking horse and the doll's house, but the wooden door had vanished. She went back to bed and cried. In a moment her father was beside her, holding her in his arms.

"What is it, darling? A bad dream?"

"I—I couldn't find something. I couldn't find some-body. I'm lost Daddy, I'm lost."

"It was a bad dream, but you're awake now. There's nothing to cry about."

"But there is, you don't understand. There's every-thing to cry about."

Her father stayed beside her, stroking her hair, till she fell asleep.

Jane felt that she'd never see Abel again. His room had vanished and when she peered into the gilt-framed mirror there were only ordinary things to see, the hall, the white staircase, and her father and mother. Noth-ing more.

Then, after she'd given up hope, she saw Abel just once more. The nights were getting lighter, and it was on her way up to bed that she stopped to look in the mirror. She felt sleepy. The glass clouded over, and then it cleared. There was Abel, in a dark hat and coat, and Patty, and a man carrying a box.

"You'll be all right," said Patty gently. "Brown will ride with you to the turnpike and put you on the coach. It'll only be a few months before you are home again."

"You'll like school," said Brown. "You'll get up to

mischief with the other young gentlemen, I'll be bound."

But Jane could see by Abel's face that he was on the verge of tears.

"Patty," he said, as she kissed him, "care for my rabbits and talk to Caesar sometimes. Don't let him forget me."

"I'll do that, Master Abel. Never fear."

Jane sprang from behind the curtain and ran out, catching Abel's arm.

"I'll write to you," she said, "really I will. And you must write to me. Where is your school? What's the address?"

At once a look of surprise, almost horror, came over the faces of Patty and Brown. Abel smiled and began to speak, but no words came except a faint "farewell."

She was alone in the hall. She looked in the mirror and knew that she would never see Abel again. She could no longer get back into that other world.

She breathed on the glass and made a misty patch. She wrote an *A* in the mist with her finger. But it soon faded. She went slowly up to bed, the mirror reflecting her bowed, fair head.

The White-haired Children

The children in the village of Cockle knew each other very well. They all went to the same school, and they bought their candy at the same shop. The same cobbler put hobnails in their thick shoes, and they had the same doctor to look after them when they were ill. They lived within a stone's throw of each other, except for a few children whose fathers were farmers, and they lived only a few fields away.

William and Mary had been born in the village, and like all their friends they knew every cottage and garden, every stream and tree. They were as surprised as everyone else when they first saw the strange, white-haired children.

It was a very hot day, and the village children were playing by the stream, some actually in the water, and others sitting on the grassy bank, dangling their feet. Suddenly William noticed a tall, fair girl standing near-by. She held two small children by the hand, and three slightly bigger ones stood behind. Each of the new family was as fair as a lily, that is, so fair that their hair was almost white.

They quietly began to take off their sandals, the little ones tugging at the tall girl's shorts as a sign that they needed some help. She unfastened buckles where necessary, and soon they were all standing in the stream.

By now, all the village children were watching the strangers. Till this moment, there had been a cheerful bustle going on, children shouting, children splashing, children singing, but now all was quiet. The new children were as silent as rushes. They moved a little, the taller ones into deeper water, but there was neither splash nor shout.

The eldest girl was called Primrose, as the little ones sometimes said her name to draw her attention to this or that. She had long, thin, white arms, and long, thin, white legs, and her face was pale, too. Her three brothers and two sisters were just the same, except that they were of different sizes and the boys had their hair cut shorter. They were all alike, wearing faded shirts and faded cotton shorts. But they did not look poor. They just looked different.

William showed one of the boys a frog and he smiled shyly. Mary showed Primrose a patch of orchids and invited her to smell them, and she smelled them and said, "Lovely." But they were not easy to talk to, and when Primrose began gathering her family to her and telling them it was time to go home, no one had found out much about them. They set off towards the hill, turning to wave white hands to the village children who waved their brown ones back.

"We ought to have asked them where they lived," said someone.

"And what their names are," added someone else.

"And if they're coming to our school."

"And how old they are."

"We know the tall girl is Primrose."

"And one of the boys is Cedar."

"And I think another sounded like Holly."

The children all hoped they would meet these new friends again and get to know them better, but they didn't turn up at school and were never seen in the village shop. They were always spoken of as "the white-haired children."

William and Mary tried asking their parents if they had seen a family with white hair, but for some reason their parents were not helpful. They seemed to think the children were teasing them, or describing some game they had played or a story they had read. But their mother said in a comforting way, "Of course we'll tell you if we see any strange white-haired children, or white-haired grown-up people, either. Of course we'll keep our eyes open and tell you."

But William and Mary knew by her tone of voice that she didn't fully believe in Primrose and Cedar and the others. She still thought they might be made-up.

It was very hot when Farmer Brown cut his hay, with not a breath of air stirring. "There'll be a storm before the hay is in," people said. "You mark our words."

On Saturday the children went to help with the hay. The shady side of the hedge was hung with rucksacks and baskets containing picnic food. The grown-up people drank cider and the children lemonade or pop. During the afternoon, when the haymakers were getting hot and tired, they suddenly noticed some strange children had joined them. The girls wore sunbonnets and the boys floppy straw hats.

"They're the white-haired children," whispered William and Mary. "Look! They've brought their hayforks and they know just how to use them. Even the tiny one has a tiny fork."

Primrose was showing this smallest one what to do. "Toss like this, Pimpernel, and don't try to turn too much at once. That's right. That's a clever girl!"

"Hello, Primrose," said Mary. "Hot, isn't it?"

"Yes," said Primrose with a quick smile, working away steadily and only pausing to look at a scratched leg, or to wipe a damp face.

"Where do you come from, little maiden?" asked Farmer Brown, in his loud, jolly voice.

"Over the hill," said Primrose, pointing to the green slope of Hunter's Hill.

"Will your father or mother be coming to fetch you home when it's time?" he went on slyly.

"Oh no, we look after ourselves, don't we, children?"

"Yes, Primrose," echoed the other five voices.

The village children felt a little envious. They loved their parents dearly, and needed them, but it might be a nice change to look after themselves when it came to deciding when to go to bed or when to go out to play.

While they had a break for tea, the white-haired children took off their hats and everyone could see their pale hair, pressed flat on their heads by the heat. The hotter they got, the whiter their skins looked, which was odd as the village children were mostly scarlet after their hard work in the hot sun.

They discovered that the third girl was called Pansy and the third boy Willow. Farmer Brown didn't give up easily and he tried to collect some more information.

"Now Primrose is a pretty name to be sure, but what comes after? What is your full name?"

"Primrose is my name and I don't need any other," said Primrose in her cool, low voice. "You are Farmer Brown and I am Primrose. Isn't that enough?" She looked bewildered and Farmer Brown said heartily, "Course it is, enough for me, anyhow. Primrose you are and Primrose you shall stay."

Before the tea-break was over, Primrose had gathered her flock around her and they started off towards Hunter's Hill, turning at intervals to wave their hayforks. The other haymakers waved back.

Haymaking lost most of its pleasure for the other children when the white-haired ones were out of sight. Squabbles broke out, and little ones complained that midges were biting them and that they were thirsty. Soon they were taken home and bathed and put to bed.

As her mother drew her curtains, Mary wondered who was putting the white-haired children to bed. She tried to imagine a tall pale lady like Primrose, only grown-up. Though Primrose was always quiet and busy with the little ones, Mary felt that she liked her. She almost felt they were friends. They had exchanged smiles and glances.

During the autumn the white-haired children appeared once, when William and Mary and some friends were picking blackberries. But while William and Mary were collecting all the berries they picked in baskets, the white-haired children were simply eating. Their faces and hands were stained purple, and they had reached the stage when only a very plump and perfect berry tempted them.

"If you eat them all, you won't have any to take home," said William severely.

"We don't need to take them home if we don't want," said Cedar.

"Then how can your mother make blackberry jelly—"

"And blackberry jam—"

"And blackberry pie—"

"And blackberry pudding—"

"Perhaps we don't want all these things," said Primrose. "Perhaps we just live on ice cream."

"And pancakes," said Pansy.

"And lollipops," said Pimpernel.

"And plum pudding," said Cedar.

"And meringues," said Holly.

"And strawberries," said Willow.

"Perhaps!" teased William. "You and your per-
hapses! Do you think we believe you? You'd have to be
princes and princesses to eat party food all year
round."

"Perhaps we are princes and princesses!"

"Perhaps! Perhaps!" mocked the village children.
"Perhaps pigs can fly."

Primrose slipped a handful of berries into Mary's
basket, and Mary whispered, "Thank you. Don't mind
what the others say. I do believe you. I always will."

"I know," said Primrose. "I know you do."

"All the same," Mary said to William as they carried
their brimming baskets home, "it must be rather fun
just to eat what you fancy, and not pick—pick—pick
—a whole afternoon, as we've done, and hardly eat
more than about six because we promised Mother we
wouldn't."

"I'd rather live in a proper home like we do," said
William, "with proper parents who know how to behave, and who know how we ought to behave. Why, I
said to Pimpernel, 'Your mother will be cross when
she sees all those squashed blackberries on your
dress,' and she said, 'Why? I'm not cross. Why should
anyone be cross?' I think it is very odd."

"Kind of odd but kind of nice," said Mary. "Nice if
no one were ever cross."

Blackberries were over, and leaves fallen, and holly
berries shining scarlet when the snow came. As the
children were going to bed, they saw the first, slow
flakes whirling past the window. The next day the

world was white. As the Christmas holidays had begun, they could play all day in the snow. Sleds were gotten down from attics and out of sheds, and dusted and examined.

Many of the sleds seemed smaller than they had the winter before.

"This can't be my sled, it's so narrow."

"I thought my sled was heavy—now it's light. I can lift it with one hand."

"There's hardly room for two on this, whatever can have happened?"

"You've grown," said the fathers and mothers. "You're a big boy now. You're a tall, strong girl. We won't need to pull you along for a treat this year as we did last."

Hunter's Hill was just right for sledding. There were short, gentle slopes near the foot where the very youngest and smallest could sled. The big ones made a snow bank across the bottom so the small sleds could come to a stop safely.

Then the middle-sized children had a longer, steeper run, starting higher up the hill, and the biggest children of all, and the most fearless, had a long, steep run right from the top to the bottom.

This long, steep run was so swift and exciting that even grown-up people used it on weekends, flashing down like an airplane about to take off. Once in motion, there was no question of stopping till the sled came to rest in the middle of the field.

William and Mary had a heavy, solid sled that had

belonged to their father when he was a boy. It was hard work dragging it up the hill, but once launched, it went like the wind. The runners were shod with iron which slid beautifully over the hard, packed snow.

The cold weather went on and on, and the children could hardly believe their eyes when every morning they saw the same crisp, even snow, and the same white roofs on the houses, and the same bright icicles on gates and railings.

William and Mary sledded all day long, only going home for meals. William sat in the front and steered, and Mary sat behind. If they changed seats, they did not get on so well. They became skillful and daring, racing all the other sleds in the middle-sized group. Sometimes they almost felt they were flying, as the polished runners skimmed so lightly over the surface of the snow, hardly seeming to touch.

The other children were full of admiration at first, stopping to watch and cheer as they flashed past, but they soon got used to the sight and took no notice except to keep out of the way.

It was a proud day when some big children, some of whom had left school, called out to William and Mary, "Would you two like to have a go on the long run down? You could manage it, judging by your present form. We'll give you a hand in dragging the sled up to the top."

William and Mary were excited and breathless when they got to the top, even though a big boy had done most of the pulling. His long strides had meant that they had to run to keep up. From the top, the run down looked difficult and dangerous. Because of the uneven hillside, there was a slow, wide curve, ending in a perfectly straight, steep finish.

"You won't find the curve too bad," said the boy. "Watch one or two other sleds first. You just have to lean before you pass the clump of bushes and brake with your foot to make sure you clear them. The rest is plain sailing—or plain sledding, if you like."

"And if you *do* land in the bushes," said a girl, "you won't be the first. I've been tipped out there lots of times. Once you get the knack, there's nothing to it."

William and Mary watched three sleds take the run with perfect success. Then it was their turn.

"Sure you'd like to have a go?"

" 'Course we're sure," said William.

"Certain sure," said Mary.

"Ready! Steady! Go!" They were given a friendly push and were off. The curve around the bushes was not as bad as it looked. Mary, with her arms around William's waist, leaned when he leaned, and straightened when he straightened, and it was only a few moments before the steep, downward run lay in front and they took it at top speed, the cold air catching their breath.

"It's the best thing I've done in my life," said William, as the sled came to rest. "It's like flying."

"How shall we get back to the top?" sighed Mary. But she need not have worried. Each time they toiled up the hill someone passing gave them a hand, and many willing hands were eager to give them a push and launch them on the downward run.

Sometimes one of them would be asked to join a team on a big sled, and though this was exciting, too, they liked their own sled best. It was so familiar that it did just what they wanted, more like something alive than an object made of wood and metal and a length of rope.

Once, plodding up the hill, Mary spoke of the white-haired children.

"I can only imagine them in the summer, can't you?" she said. "But I suppose there must be snow on the other side of the hill, where they live, and they're sure to be playing in it like us. They'll need several sleds for the six of them. But perhaps Pimpernel and Willow aren't big enough to sled yet. I expect Primrose pulls them along for a ride. She's like a mother."

"She isn't really," said William, "because she doesn't mind what they do and mothers are always minding about something or other."

"But she keeps an eye on them, doesn't she?"

"Yes, in a way. But not a mother's eye."

The very next day the white-haired children appeared on the village side of Hunter's Hill. There they were, all six of them, with fur hats and fur mittens, each with his or her own sled painted scarlet. Primrose's was the biggest, then Cedar's, then Pansy's, then Holly's, right down to little Willow and Pimpernel who had sleds almost doll size.

The little ones joined the group of youngest children, the middle-sized ones the middle group, and

Primrose and Cedar climbed confidently to the top of the long run.

"Can you manage it?" asked one of the leaders among the big boys.

"It's faster than you think."

"And there's the bend by the bushes."

"There's no hope of braking when you're under way. You just have to sit tight and hope for the best."

"It's kind of you to take so much trouble," said Primrose, "but my brother and I are quite safe. Why, on the other side of the hill, we have a much longer run with three bends—sharp ones—and a steep finish like the side of a house. This is easy as pie compared with the other."

"Very well. Please yourselves. We only wanted to help."

The group of older children went on talking and paying no more attention to the newcomers, but when Primrose got her sled in position, every eye was quietly fixed on her. She lay on her sled, pulled her fur hat farther down on her head, and kicked off.

Down the run she sped, curving around the bushes, on till she reached the last steep pitch.

"Well done!" said some of the watchers when she returned. "I wouldn't be surprised if you've beaten the record for speed."

The white-haired children were all experts, and very willing to lend their sleds and accept turns on other people's. Although Mary never said more to Primrose than, "Have a go on mine" or, "Shall we both try a run on yours?" she felt they were getting to know each other. William and Cedar, too, were like old friends without many words being spoken. If Primrose were late, Mary felt unsettled till she came, and when Primrose had gone home, the best of the day's fun seemed over. The two boys felt the same about each other.

One day, Mary was surprised when Primrose drew her aside and said, "We are giving a party. Will you and your brother come?"

"Yes, we'd love to. That is, if Mother says we may. When is it to be?"

"Actually it's tonight, when we go home."

"I'll ask mother at lunch time and tell you this afternoon. But perhaps you won't be coming this afternoon as you'll be getting things ready for the party."

"Oh, we shall come. There's nothing to get ready. But please don't ask your mother. Please don't. She might say no."

"Why should she?"

"Children think we are queer, and grown-up people think we are very queer indeed. We have queer names and peculiar hair, and we look after ourselves. Please don't ask permission. Just come, both of you."

"But we mustn't be late back. Mother would worry terribly if it got pitch dark and we weren't home."

"Would she think you'd been eaten by wolves, or stolen by robbers?"

Mary wasn't sure if Primrose were serious or teasing.

"Not exactly," she said. "She'd just worry. You know how mothers worry."

"I don't, but never mind. We'll leave earlier than usual, before the sun sets, and we'll sled down the other side of the hill, and the sled run ends at our front door. Do, please come. We want you and William 'specially. As a matter of fact, we've arranged a surprise for you. Just for you."

"What about our clothes?"

"Everyone will come in sledding clothes because they'll come on sleds. So you'll come? And please don't mention it to any of the other children because we're not asking anyone else from this village."

"Yes, we'll come. I'll go and ask William now."

William was not even anxious about getting home in good time. He just said yes. The idea of going in sledding clothes was an added attraction. No washings of neck or knees, or nonsense about clean nails. A party after his own heart.

That afternoon, when the red sun ball was still above the horizon, Primrose began collecting her family together, and William and Mary joined them. They followed a path leading around the side of the hill, and when they were right around to the opposite side, they struck the top of the sled run Primrose had described.

"I'll go first," said Primrose. "Then you, Mary, with William. Then Cedar, and then the little ones can come as they please. Don't be frightened if you go rather fast because it's quite, quite safe; there's only one way home from here, and you can't get lost. Just be careful when you go through the gates of the drive. Of course the gates will be wide open, but you don't want to hit a gatepost."

She got ready on her sled.

"The next person had better count ten slowly before pushing off. That ought to prevent any accidents. Ten slowly—don't forget!"

"Ten slowly—we won't forget."

Then, in a flash, Primrose was off down the hillside.

It was several seconds before William and Mary remembered to begin counting, and they counted rather quickly for fear that Primrose would be out of sight. When they pushed off, she was still visible, a moving dot swinging around a curve.

It was a wonderful sled run, polished and smooth, with the bends banked so the sled slid around with no worry about steering or braking. The sled was out of their control, but they never doubted they would end up at the right place. After the first steep rush, the run flattened out and they saw the gateposts as they slipped between them, then down a drive where two rows of snowy trees met in a series of arches. Then the front of a great house sprang up, brilliantly lit.

It must be a palace, thought Mary, gazing up at the rows of bright windows. Doors were open into the hall, and the light streamed out upon the sparkling snow.

The courtyard was packed with sleds of all sizes and colors and kinds, some expensive and new, some homemade and old. The rest of the white-haired children arrived, one by one, and many other children. These must have come from other villages, as they were strangers.

"Come in, everybody!" said Primrose, from the open door. "Go where you like. Do what you like. The whole house is ours tonight, every nook and cranny. Come in and make yourselves at home. We only want to please you."

At first the guests were shy, and stood about in the hall where there was a blazing log fire. Then some of the bolder ones began to explore, opening a door here, going up a few stairs with their hand on the banister, and at last swarming everywhere, upstairs, downstairs, in attics and cellars, peeping in cupboards and on shelves.

There were games laid out in some rooms. Toys in others. Puzzles and tricks in others. Music came from a room cleared for dancing, and there was even a quiet room with books lying around. The smallest children found their way to a nursery and were soon riding rocking horses and building with bricks the size of real ones, but light to handle. Little girls played with a dolls' house or busied themselves putting dolls to bed in cots and cradles, with a musical box to play a lullaby.

William played darts with some other boys, and Mary found a box of beads, all the colors of the rainbow, with a label on the box which said, PLEASE MAKE WHAT YOU LIKE AND TAKE IT HOME WITH YOU.

She began to thread herself a necklace, using the crystal beads which sparkled like the frost outside. Sometimes Primrose put her head around the door, smiling and nodding, but did not stay.

Everyone was laughing, and many were shouting and racing around, but the house was so large that the party did not seem noisy. It did not seem crowded,

either, with so many rooms for the guests to use and
so many different things for them to do. When a loud
gong sounded, there was a rush for the stairs and the
dining room, where a round table was spread with a
white cloth and covered with delicious food. Whatever
any child liked best was sure to be there, whether it
was pancakes or peaches, sausages or strawberries,
lobster or lollipops. The children moved around helping themselves to whatever took their fancy.

In the middle of the table was a wonderful frozen
pudding, like a mountain made of snowy ice cream. At
the top was a sled with two tiny figures on it, a boy and
a girl. They looked as though, any minute, they would
start their run down the mountainside where a winding track was clearly marked. This track went in and
out of silvery fir trees, down to the valley below and
over a bridge which spanned a stream.

"When do we eat the iced pudding?" asked someone.

"Last thing of all," said Primrose, "not till it's time
to go home. When the pudding is eaten, the party is
over."

Mary could not take her eyes off the iced mountain,
and while she ate boats made of celery with lettuce
sails, she stared and stared.

She knew that some very skilled cook had made this
wonderful dessert, yet she felt it was more than just a
pudding for a party. It was a real scene of snow and ice
and frosty trees and sparkling water. The bridge had a
handrail at one side and the snow on it was scuffled. It

looked as if some passerby had gripped it to steady himself. Then she saw something else that made her open her eyes even wider.

"William," whispered Mary, "William, look at the children on the sled."

William leaned forward so his eyes were level with the top of the pudding and the sled.

"They're very well made," he said.

"But don't you see who they are—don't you recognize them? Look properly!"

William looked again. "Goodness, they're you and me! Your blue cap and my red, our navy wind-jackets and your red pants and my brown. They're us, all right. But why doesn't someone else notice? It's so obvious."

"It's obvious to us, of course, but not many people here have ever seen us before. And lots of children wear clothes very like ours when they sled."

"But not *exactly* like ours! You agree that it couldn't possibly be just chance? Someone meant it. Someone took a great deal of trouble to get it right. Why, even your hair is darker than mine!"

"Ought we to thank Primrose?"

"I'm not sure. She hasn't mentioned it to us. When we go, we can just say we thought the pudding was marvelous, or something like that."

"All right," said Mary. "Everything is so strange tonight, I feel anything could happen. It's this huge house and all these children and no one looking after us."

"I'm going back upstairs," said William. "I saw a

room with a model railway simply covering the whole floor, with stations and bridges and tunnels. I'm going to play with it."

He ran off, and Mary, who was wearing her crystal necklace, followed. She went into a room where music was being played and children were dancing. At once a boy in a kilt asked her to be his partner.

"Do you live far away?" he asked.

"Just over the hill," said Mary.

"So do I. Isn't it funny, we all come from just over the hill, but I don't think it can be the same hill, do you?"

"No, it can't be, or we should all know each other. Did you come on a sled?"

"Yes, like everyone else."

As they danced near the platform Mary noticed that the musicians were all children, too. She felt sure it must be getting late and she said good-bye to her partner and went to look for William. She met him on the landing, looking for her.

"Should we go?" said Mary. "It feels late."

"Yes, it does, and there aren't any clocks in this place. I've looked especially. I asked Primrose what the time was and she just said, 'Still very early—you mustn't dream of going yet.'"

They sat down on a window seat, half hidden by heavy red curtains, and looked down onto the courtyard with its rows and rows of sleds. They picked out their own, near to the stone steps leading to the front door. Just then, they heard Primrose's voice speaking quietly to Cedar.

"Not long to wait now," she said.

"But I haven't seen William and Mary lately," said Cedar.

"Oh, they're still here. William was getting anxious about the time, but I told him it was still early."

"Have they noticed anything?"

"I don't think they have. They haven't said anything. Oh, won't it be lovely to have them here always, to play with whenever we want?"

"Yes, it will be fun, but we mustn't be too sure. I feel that something could go wrong even now. They might escape."

"No! No! No!" said Primrose. "It will be all right— you'll see. I'll sound the gong now, this minute, and then we'll serve the iced pudding. When that's gone, they won't be able to get back!"

"No, they won't. There won't be a way back!"

William and Mary heard the other two running towards the stairs.

"We must get away as quickly as we can," said William. "We haven't a minute to lose."

"I don't understand—but I'm frightened," said Mary.

Just then the gong sounded and there was a mad rush towards the dining room, the children all calling out, as they ran, "Now for the iced pudding! The iced pudding is to be served now! Come along, everyone, and have your share!"

William and Mary wanted to go through the hall, but the press of children carried them along, willynilly, into the dining room.

Primrose stood by the table with a large silver spoon, calling out as she scooped it into the mountainside, "Hold out your plates! A helping for everyone!"

When they saw the spoon buried in the pudding, and the sled with its tiny occupants poised on the top, William and Mary knew that they must be out of the house in a matter of seconds. They tore on their boots, dashed out of the door, snatched up the rope on their sled and ran. They did not look back once at the house with its lighted windows, but ran faster than they had ever run before. Only at the top of the hill they paused and looked back. The landscape behind was completely different. Sloping hillside, trees, track, all had disappeared. There was only a blank stretch of snow.

"Just in time," said William. "Now for the homeward run."

When they arrived at their own home, their parents were not cross or alarmed. They smiled and remarked that the children must have had an extra good time playing as they were rather late.

"We sledded on the other side of the hill,'" said William.

"And went home with some children we knew."

"You look tired, anyhow," said their mother. "I'll read to you while you have your supper."

"We've had supper—" began William, but by then she had fetched *Robinson Crusoe* from the shelf, taken out the marker, and begun to read, while the children tried to manage at least their cocoa and a toasted tea cake.

As they went to bed, they planned, at the very first chance, to visit the white-haired children again, and to see what the house looked like in daylight. But it was to be several months before they were able to do this.

That night the thaw set in, and there was no more playing in the snow—only slogging along in the slush. Then school started again and whenever they suggested a Sunday walk right over Hunter's Hill, their father said it was private land, and they had better not go without permission.

It was not till summer that their chance came. An older cousin came to stay, a tall boy almost grown-up. He was willing to explore on the other side of the hill, striding off at such a pace that they had to run to keep up with him.

The hill was green now, with sheep on the higher slopes and buttercups at the bottom. As they went down, they searched the landscape for a big house, but they searched in vain.

"We're looking for a house we once went to," said William.

"A house as big as a palace," said Mary, "with stone gateposts and a drive."

"And the trees in the drive had branches meeting to make arches."

"Can't see a thing!" said the cousin, "not even a cow shed. Sounds like a fairy tale to me. But we'll walk on for another quarter of an hour and then we'll turn back."

Before this quarter of an hour was up they came to a pair of old, stone gateposts, green with moss. Beyond was an overgrown drive, thick with weeds. Several trees had fallen right across it, and others had lost branches in storms.

"I suppose this isn't what you were looking for?" laughed the cousin. "Let's go up the drive, anyway."

They climbed over the fallen trees and scrambled over the dead branches, scratching their legs while their feet sank deep in a thick, soft carpet of decaying leaves. A startled bird rose with a cry and made them jump. Then they came to the house, or what had once been the house. It was a ruin, with no glass in the windows, the doors swinging on broken hinges, and great, gaping holes in the roof. Nettles and docks grew in the hall, and the window sills were hung with ivy.

"If we had more time, we'd go in and explore," said

the cousin, but neither William nor Mary wanted to set foot over that doorstep again. They knew that whatever was inside, they would not find the white-haired children.

They were silent on the way home, but the cousin did not notice as he was not used to children, and did not know what to say to them anyway. He left them to their own disturbing, puzzling thoughts.

As they changed their shoes for tea, William whispered to Mary, "Was it all a dream?"

Mary whispered back, "How can you say that? You know it wasn't. It really happened. Anyhow, I still have the crystal necklace I threaded. That's proof, isn't it?"

"We've lots to ask Primrose if we ever see her again."

"Yes, we have. She must have wondered what went wrong with her plan, and why we ran away when we did."

But the white-haired children never visited the village of Cockle again, though William and Mary looked for them by the river and in the hayfield, and among the blackberry bushes, and most of all on Hunter's Hill when the snow came and sledding began again.

About the Author

Ruth Ainsworth is married, with three sons, now grown up. When her children were small and living in the country, they demanded stories. She says, "I made up endless stories as we went on endless walks, often windy and wintry, and *they* told *me* wonderful stories, too!"

Ms. Ainsworth is well known in England as a writer for young children. Besides her published stories, much of her work has been broadcast by the BBC on their programs for children. Several of her stories have been televised as puppet plays.